THE DOCTORS' BABY BOND

BY
ABIGAIL GORDON

MILLS & BOON®

First published in Great Britain 2005
Large Print edition 2005
Harlequin Mills & Boon Limited,
Eton House, 18-24 Paradise Road,
Richmond, Surrey TW9 1SR

© Abigail Gordon 2005

ISBN 0 263 18474 9

Set in Times Roman 16½ on 17½ pt.
17-0805-47354

Printed and bound in Great Britain
by Antony Rowe Ltd, Chippenham, Wiltshire

CHAPTER ONE

AT LAST golden lashes were drooping onto tiny cheeks and Andrina gave a sigh of relief. Just as she'd thought she was getting her act together after a month of sleepless nights, interminable feeds and domestic chaos, the little one in her arms had reminded her that complacency was not on the agenda in their present circumstances.

He'd had a digestive upset that had made him fretful and restless and only now did the discomfort seem to be subsiding. She'd sent for the doctor, feeling that another opinion besides her own was needed, and had been reassured when told that it should clear up satisfactorily if the baby was given just water for a few hours. But during that time there had been hungry protests from the small patient and she'd cuddled him constantly through the night until sleep had come.

As she laid him in his cot Andrina was conscious of the mess around her. The sink was full of dirty pots, her own bed was unmade and a glimpse of herself in the bathroom mirror said that her appearance fitted in with the general state of chaos in the apartment.

A white, tired face looked back at her from beneath tousled brown hair and she could see the panic that the baby's sudden illness had brought still present in red-rimmed hazel eyes.

He was such a helpless little scrap she couldn't bear to see him in pain, but hopefully sleep would help to calm down the digestive upset and he might be more peaceful when he woke up.

As she continued to stare at the face in the mirror, tears welled up in the tired eyes looking back at her. During the last few days she'd been congratulating herself that she was finally on top of everything. That after the terrible shock on that hot and airless night in July she was coping. She *had* been, until the previous evening when it had all gone haywire.

She would have a cup of tea and then start the big tidy-up, she told herself, brushing away the tears. It was no use crying. There was no one to know or care about what was happening to her. She just had to get on with it for the baby's sake.

She was drooping over the sink, waiting for the kettle to fill, when the doorbell rang, and as the health visitor was the only person likely to be calling on her she opened the door expecting it to be her, but it wasn't.

A tall man with golden hair and eyes as blue as delphiniums was standing on the mat outside her high-rise apartment. He looked clean, fresh and smart, and Andrina thought that whatever it was he was selling she wished she didn't look such a mess. But was she in the mood for pleasantries? No.

'Yes?' she questioned, thinking longingly of the pot of tea she'd been about to make.

He smiled and she thought irritably that this man looked as if he hadn't a care in the world, while she was bogged down with responsibilities.

'I'm looking for Andrina Bell,' he said with the smile still in place. 'Would you happen to be her?'

'I might be,' she said warily, hiding her surprise. 'What is it that you want?'

'My name is Drew Curtis. I'm a doctor in general practice and am trying to trace an ex-employee of mine, Jodie Stewart. I believe that you are her next of kin. At least, that is what it says on her records at the surgery.'

Andrina was goggling at him in amazement.

'You're looking for J-Jodie,' she stuttered. This was bizarre!

'Yes. I have a responsibility towards her. I need to know if she is all right. I've got ID and here's proof that I know her.' He showed her an identity card and then took a small photograph from his inside pocket. It was of himself and another similar-looking man, both with their arms around a smiling Jodie.

She stepped back.

'You'd better come in,' she said woodenly, 'and, please, don't make a noise.'

'Er, right, thank you,' he said, lowering his voice and looking puzzled at the same time. 'I hope I'm not intruding.'

Oh, he was intruding all right, she thought, and whether it was a good omen or bad she wasn't sure. Someone who'd actually known her stepsister had appeared out of the blue and he was in for a shock. Her heart was thudding in her chest. He had the same colouring as the baby. Was he the father?

He was looking around him, the stranger who had come to her door, and she thought that he couldn't help but notice what a mess the place was and that her face was blotched with the tears she'd just shed.

'Jodie was pregnant when she left the practice where we were employing her as a receptionist,' he said. 'She left us to go and live in London and I visited her a couple of times there as I was concerned about her welfare. But when I went there recently, knowing that she was soon to give birth, I found that all the flats in the building were empty, scheduled for demolition, and no one could tell me where she'd gone. That is why I've come to you.'

'Are you the father of her child?' Andrina asked through lips that had gone dry as desert dust.

She could see where this was leading. When this Dr Curtis person heard what she had to say he would stake his claim and break her heart at the same time.

She watched his jaw sag at the question.

'Why do you ask? Hasn't she told you what happened?' he said flatly.

'When I last saw Jodie we hadn't spoken in a long time,' Andrina told him, 'and by that time it was too late to talk. She was dead.'

'Dead!' he echoed. 'Jodie dead!' His face was bleached with horror. 'How? Why? And what about the baby?'

'He was delivered by Caesarean section just before she died. If you want to see him, he's asleep in the next room. But, please, don't disturb him. He's been unwell and I've only just got him to sleep after a long weary night.'

*   *   *

It had been nearing the end of a hot, airless day in July when the phone call that had changed her life had come through. Thunder had been rumbling in the distance and as it had come closer Andrina had thrown off the bed covers and padded across to the window to watch the lightning flash across the sky.

She'd been tired when she'd got in, ready to fall into bed and sleep the night away, but it had seemed as if there had been no air and oblivion had been hard to come by.

When the phone had rung she'd groaned. She was not going back to the hospital for anything or anyone, she'd thought as she'd picked up the receiver. Not even for the head of the trust himself. She'd put in more than her share of hours and now needed the rest if she was to perform tomorrow as well as she'd done today.

It was well known in hospital circles that if Andrina Bell, or 'Ding Dong' as she was known to some of the less reverent amongst them, didn't get a good night's sleep, woe betide those who didn't please her the next day. But the phone call was to change all that.

It *was* a hospital on the line, but not the one where she was employed. A woman's voice with all the right inflexions required of the bearer of bad news said in her ear, 'This is the accident and emergency department of a hospital in London. I need to speak to Andrina Bell.'

'Speaking,' she said in terse surprise.

She'd been applying for jobs recently, stacks of them, but couldn't remember anything in the London area, and in any case they'd been vacancies in general practice as she was ready for a change of direction and had recently been training towards that end, with short stints in some local practices.

'I have your name as next of kin to a Jodie Stewart. Is that correct?' the voice had said in the same careful tones.

If she'd been wilting with the heat before, now her legs were turning to jelly because of what the woman was saying.

'Yes. I am the next of kin to Jodie Stewart,' she told her. 'She's my stepsister. What's wrong?'

'She was in a road accident earlier this evening. Lost control of her car and ran into a tree. Jodie is in a critical condition. She managed to give us some details when she was first brought in here, but since then her condition has worsened and that is why I'm contacting you.'

'How critical?' she'd asked hoarsely.

'Very. I would suggest that you come immediately if you want to see her...er...'

'Alive? I'm a doctor,' she'd told the woman. 'So you don't need to pull your punches. Just give me the address and I'll be on my way within minutes.'

'You're Gloucester-based, aren't you?' the unwelcome caller had said. 'So you should be with us in two or three hours. I'll have someone be on the lookout for you, Dr Bell.'

As she'd driven through the humid night, her exhaustion forgotten, Andrina's thoughts had gone back to their childhood, and they weren't happy thoughts. Her mother, a hitherto sensible widow, had married again when Andrina had been in her early teens.

She'd met Morgan Stewart, a Shakespearean actor type, himself a widower with a small daughter, and had been infatuated from the start, resulting in Andrina having been constantly in charge of little Jodie while the lovebirds had played at being Romeo and Juliet.

Wherever she'd gone, the little one had tagged along, demanding, cajoling, taking up all her free time, and she'd often thought dismally that her new stepfather hadn't just gained himself a wife, he'd acquired a childminder, too.

Andrina had escaped when she'd left home to go to medical school and some years later Jodie had done the same, but not to take up a career. She'd flitted from job to job, and as the two girls had never been close in their adult lives, Andrina hadn't known half the time what her stepsister had been up to.

Their parents, now elderly, lived in Spain, where her mother was devotedly looking after

Morgan after a serious stroke. There was no way they could offer any help or support, hence the fact that Jodie had given Andrina's name as next of kin instead of her father's.

When Andrina arrived at the intensive care section of the hospital where her stepsister had been taken, a nurse greeted her, and Andrina knew from her expression that she was too late.

'I'm so sorry,' she said, 'Jodie died half an hour ago. We did our best but her injuries were too severe for there to be any hope of recovery. If you'll come this way, I'll take you to see her. That is, if you feel up to it. You look exhausted. Maybe a cup of tea first would be a good idea.'

Andrina shook her head.

'No, take me to her, please. I need to say my goodbyes.'

She sat for a long time beside Jodie's still figure, filled with regret that they hadn't even been able to say their farewells after all the wasted years. She thought sadly that they were spending more time together in death than they'd done in life for many a long year, and now all that lay ahead was a long and final silence.

When at last she left Jodie's side, the nurse was hovering and she said gently, 'You haven't mentioned the baby, so I take it that when they phoned you weren't told that we were able to save it.'

'Baby!' Andrina choked as her legs gave way beneath her.

'I'm right, then,' the other woman said sympathetically as she helped Andrina to a chair. 'You weren't aware that your sister was pregnant, were you?'

Dazed and incredulous, she shook her head. It would seem that this night of horrors wasn't over.

'The person who phoned to tell you about the accident must have thought that you would have enough to think about, driving all that way, without being told there was a newborn baby awaiting your arrival. Your sister gave birth to a beautiful little boy just before she died,' the nurse said in a voice that sounded to

Andrina as if it was coming from far away. 'We had to do a Caesarean but he's fine. I'll take you to see him.'

'No! Yes!' she groaned. 'I can't take it in. Jodie is dead and she's left a baby. You're right. I didn't know she was pregnant. What am I going to do? I'm a busy doctor living in a high-rise apartment.'

The nurse took her hand and as Andrina got slowly to her feet she said, 'Just come and look at him and you'll be grateful that you've got something to remember her by. Jodie has left a new generation to care for.'

'How can I do it?' she'd sobbed. 'I can't! I just can't!'

But when she saw him, with the redness and wrinkles of the newly born, lying defenceless in the bassinet where they'd placed him, there hadn't really been any decision to make. Her heart had made it for her. Whether she wanted to or not, and even though she was under no legal obligation, she had to take care of Jodie's child.

*   *   *

'Of course I want to see him,' Drew Curtis said raggedly, and she knew with a sinking feeling that either he was a very caring employer or he had some sort of claim on the little one that she had committed herself to caring for on that dreadful night.

As he stood looking down at Jodie's child, she could see a resemblance not only in their colouring but in their features, too. Her unease was increasing. What was he here for?

Her eyes widened. The tears coursing down his face indicated that he was more than a caring employer...and he hadn't answered her question.

'*Are* you the baby's father?' she repeated.

'No,' he choked. 'I'm not.'

'Then what *is* your connection with my stepsister?' Andrina asked, as her unease began to subside.

'This baby is my brother's child.'

'Oh.'

The feeling of impending doom was back.

'And so where is *he*? Why wasn't he there to support her? Where is this surgery where you employed Jodie?'

'The answer to your first two questions is that Jonathan is dead. He died from leukaemia when she was six months pregnant. He was my junior partner in the practice. The two of them were madly in love, and when the illness, which progressed rapidly, took him, she couldn't bear to stay in the place where they'd been so happy.

'She went to live in London. I begged her not to go as I was concerned about both her physical and mental state, but she wouldn't listen. Just packed her bags and went, leaving me with the address of a flat that she'd found. So you can imagine how I felt when I went to her place last time and found the whole complex empty. I wanted to be there for her. To make up in part for Jonathan not being around. Didn't you wonder who the father of her child might be?'

'Yes, of course I did,' Andrina told him, motioning for them to go back into the other room so they didn't wake the baby up. 'But since the night she was killed in a road accident, *my* life has been turned upside down. I've

had to take leave from my job and seem to do
nothing but make feeds, keep up with his laun-
dry and try to get some sleep.

'This is nothing like I had my life planned,'
she told him wearily, 'but I had no choice.
Jodie and I were never close, due to reasons
that I won't bore you with, but when I knew
about the baby my responsibilities were clear-
cut, and ever since I brought her child home
with me I've lived from one day to the next.
Trying to cope as best I can, both physically
and financially, as I've had to take extended
leave from my job.'

'And what might that be?'

She smiled for the first time since she'd
opened the door to him, and he thought that
under less pressure she would be an attractive
woman with her slenderness and the brown
hair and hazel eyes.

'It would seem that we have *two* things in
common,' Andrina told him. 'The baby and
our occupations. At the present time I'm employed as a registrar in a hospital not far from
here. Although that was about to change as

I've been doing some general practice training, with the intention of becoming a GP.'

There was surprise in the eyes meeting hers, and she thought grimly that, looking around this place, he must be thinking heaven help her patients if this was how she lived.

But did she care what he thought? It was comforting to know that there was someone else concerned about the welfare of Jodie's child, but she didn't want him to overdo it. Apart from Morgan, he was the baby's only blood relation, while her own connection was merely through her mother's marriage to Jodie's father. So this Drew Curtis person had a prior claim to him if he should decide to do something about it.

'So we're both in health care,' he said slowly. 'That *is* a coincidence.'

'Yes, isn't it?' she agreed listlessly, and yawned.

'I feel that you'd like me to go,' he said getting to his feet.

Andrina felt her colour rise and said apologetically, 'I'm just tired, that's all. I was gasping for a cup of tea when you came. Would you like to join me?'

'Er…yes, thank you, and then I *will* go. But you will be hearing from me again once I've gathered my wits after the shock of finding that my small nephew has already arrived in the world.'

As she rummaged around for two clean cups, Andrina thought that was ominous. What he'd just said had the overtones of a solicitor's letter.

There was silence in the room as they drank the tea, each of them with their own thoughts. When Drew had put his cup down, he got to his feet, his glance on the closed door of the bedroom.

'I'd like to see the baby just once more, if I may. I promise not to disturb him.' His voice had thickened. 'I still can't take it in that in there we have all that is left of the hopes and dreams of two young people. We have been left with a great responsibility, you and I. We're going to have to decide how we're going to cope with it.'

'I'm already coping,' she told him coolly, immediately on the defensive, because at that moment it didn't look like it, with a sink full of dirty pots and an unmade bed in the room where he'd met his nephew for the first time. '*My* decision was made on a hot July night a month ago and, jaded though I am, nothing is going to change it.'

'Yes, well, we'll have to see, won't we?' he said equably, and the uncertainty that had been all around her ever since she'd discovered who he was increased.

As he was leaving he paused in the doorway and offered her his card.

'That's me,' he said. 'Drew Curtis, GP, along with my address and phone number. I have a practice in a Derbyshire village and live in an old farmhouse, which I'm renovating. If you need me for anything at all, do, please, get in touch. But I *have* said that I'll be back, and I never say anything I don't mean.'

When he'd gone Andrina sat staring into nothing. In the space of an hour her life had changed dramatically again. Out of the blue had come a man with golden hair and blue eyes, tall, straight and purposeful, and back there in the bedroom was a child whose presence had brought him into her life.

He'd wept, she thought wonderingly, the stranger who had come to her door, and had not been ashamed of it, but he'd had cause to if what he'd said was true. That his dead brother was the baby's father.

Obviously a man who took his responsibilities seriously, he'd walked into her life and told her in no uncertain terms that he wasn't going to go away.

Her thoughts switched to Jodie. She herself had been the achiever out of the two of them, but her stepsister had managed something that she hadn't. Jodie had known the joys and delights of real love, which was more than she herself ever had.

She'd had a couple of relationships over the last few years but they hadn't come to anything. Her hours and the fact that her vitality was always low had put the blight on them and they'd ended with no regret on either side.

And now she was involved in the aftermath of somebody else's love affair and, where she'd just begun to feel that she was getting her act together, now she was on shifting sands again.

It was a relief to have someone else in the baby's life, especially if this GP from Derbyshire was willing to be supportive. But just how supportive was he planning to be?

If he wanted to take the baby from her, he would have a fight on his hands. After her first shock and dismay at finding that Jodie had left a child to be cared for, she'd grown to love the tiny helpless scrap who had turned her life upside down.

But the future was still unsorted. Soon she would have to go back to work. They had to eat. Bills had to be paid. The leave she'd been granted couldn't go on for ever.

She got to her feet with new purpose. Time to worry about today's unexpected caller if he came back, and as he'd told her that he wasn't in the habit of saying things he didn't mean, no doubt he *would* be back.

As she cleared the cluttered sink and made her bed, Andrina was thinking that it was typical that she should meet one of the most attractive men she'd seen in ages under such circumstances.

On the rare occasions she'd spoken to Jodie in recent years the younger girl had always had some comment to make about Andrina's almost non-existent social life, and she'd always told Jodie that the job left little time for living it up. Now she had even less.

What was this village practice of his like? she wondered. Twenty years behind the times? She doubted it. Drew had looked cool and efficient, yet with a tolerant sort of mouth, and there was no doubt in her mind that he'd loved his brother. He must have been fond of Jodie, too, she thought, remembering his tears as he'd looked down at the sleeping baby.

As Drew drove back to where he'd come from, his mind was working overtime. He'd been dumbstruck to find that Jodie's baby had already been born and that the infant had neither mother nor father.

The pale-faced doctor back there was doing her best, but didn't seem to be coping very well. Though the baby had looked well cared for. Yet he didn't want his brother's child to be brought up in a high-rise apartment, not when there was all that clear country air back home.

But having only just met the woman and child, he wasn't exactly in a position to start reorganising their lives. She'd soon let him know that she was in charge and it was all credit to her that she was, but *he* had to do something to help. Financially certainly, but that wouldn't be enough to wipe out his concern for his orphaned nephew.

It was strange that Andrina Bell should be a doctor too *and* had done some training in general practice. He wondered how good she was. He was looking for someone to replace his brother and she could quite possibly fit the bill.

But practice matters would have to be put aside for the moment. Back there in Gloucestershire was a situation that would be for ever on his mind unless he did something about it. But what?

Back at Whistler's Farm, the once derelict place that he was halfway through renovating, Drew paced around its spacious rooms, comparing them to Andrina Bell's small apartment, and with every glance around the farmhouse's warm and welcoming interior the certainty grew that this was where the baby in the cluttered bedroom should be.

He shook his head. He'd only just got back from visiting them. He needed to sleep on it. The woman and child had managed so far without any assistance from him. Another couple of days wouldn't make much difference, and the ideas crowding his mind could stay there for a while until he'd thought them all through.

After a sleepless night he felt that he *had* considered all the options. Nothing had changed during the dark hours, except that the desire to do something for his brother's baby was increasing by the moment.

When the phone rang early the next morning Andrina found herself tensing. Calls were not that frequent and she thought immediately that it was Drew wasting no time.

When she picked up the receiver she found that it wasn't. The personnel officer from the hospital where she was employed was on the line, asking if she had any idea when she would be coming back.

'I know that you have a problem while you are looking after your sister's baby,' he said, 'but, Dr Bell, you are needed here. As you must be aware, we have a crèche for the use of mothers with small children. Maybe you could avail yourself of that facility during working hours.'

'I may do that in the future,' she told him stiffly, 'but my stepsister's baby is only four weeks old. He needs me and I couldn't bear to be away from him while he's so small. I'm having to juggle my life around and it isn't easy.'

'So do I take it that it's a no for the present?' he questioned.

'Yes, but I will come back as soon as I possibly can. I have no choice. I'm going to need the money.'

'Very well,' he agreed coolly. 'We'll give it another few weeks.'

When he'd gone off the line she stood immobile in the apartment's small hallway, thinking that it would still be the same when he rang again. She wouldn't want to leave the baby, who was for the time being legally in her care…and it was time that the little orphaned one had a name. But more important than that was the realisation that if she stayed away from the hospital for too long, she could lose her job.

Drew didn't ring, as she'd half expected. He appeared in person again late that evening, and when she opened the door to him Andrina was thankful that this time the place was tidy.

He'd had a busy day. James, the trainee doctor he was employing at the surgery, had been at college all day and Drew had done both surgeries and all the home visits. He was missing Jonathan in every way, and not least at the surgery.

If he'd had no time to think about Andrina and the baby during the day, the moment he'd finished work it had been there again, the need to do something constructive that had kept him pacing his house the night before.

The hazel-eyed woman who'd taken the child into her care couldn't do it round the clock for ever. She had a job to hold onto and what would she do when she had to go back? He didn't want to think of his nephew fobbed off onto just anyone.

When she opened the door to him for a second time there was only moderate surprise in her expression, and he thought incredulously that she'd been expecting him.

'Dr Curtis,' she said evenly, to disguise a fast beating heart. 'So soon.'

'Er…yes. I don't let the grass grow under my feet,' he said crisply, ignoring the mild sarcasm. 'I have a proposition to put to you.'

Andrina took a deep breath. This was it, she thought. He was going to exert his rights. Tell her that *he* had legal right to the baby…and that *she* could visit.

'You're not taking him away from me,' she cried, before he could say anything further.

'Whoa!' he remonstrated. 'Did I say that? I was about to explain that I would like the baby to be brought up in the place where Jonathan and I had a happy childhood. Where there are fields and clean fresh air and where one isn't a faceless person to those one meets, but part of a community.'

'It's the same thing you're suggesting,' she insisted hotly. 'You're just describing it in a different way. It won't work. I am not giving Jonathan up!'

'So he's got a name, has he?' he said in slow surprise. 'Since when?'

'Since I knew that was what his father was called. It seemed fitting…if you are in agreement.'

'Of course I am,' he told her huskily. 'I think it's a wonderful idea.'

'Good,' she told him flatly, 'but let's get back to what you were saying.'

'I will if you'll give me the chance.'

'Go ahead, then, but don't expect me to agree.'

'I want you both to come and stay with me. I've got plenty of room and I could share the burden of looking after, er...Jonathan.'

He saw amazed disbelief in her eyes as she listened to what he was saying. It was the last thing she'd been expecting him to say and instead of answering immediately she sidetracked him by saying, 'But what about your family? Are they going to want a strange woman and child foisted on them?'

'When did I say I had a family?' he commented levelly. 'You are jumping to conclusions...and not telling me what you think of my suggestion. The village is a beautiful place. Fresh and clean with friendly folk living there.'

Andrina was not to be appeased.

'Maybe, but what role would I be expected to play? Second fiddle to you?'

The idea had its appeal from one angle, but was this a ploy to get the baby on his home ground as a first step to wanting him for himself?

'Your role would be that of his stand-in mother, as it is now, and I would be someone sharing the work and responsibility in a paternal role.'

'And that's it?'

'Well…yes. What did you think I had in mind?'

'You're a blood relative and I'm not. Need I say more?'

His face was sombre.

'That may be so, but I'm fully aware that without you Jonathan would have been taken into care if Social Services couldn't find the father. Your sister and my brother have a lot to thank you for…and so have I. So how about it? You could wave this cramped place goodbye and with someone else to assist you could take up employment again in some form or other.'

Her smile was wry.

'Such as what, in a country village? Milking the cows. Haymaking?'

His answering smile had reproof in it.

'Don't knock it. Both those occupations can be very rewarding. But I was referring to the surgery. We're a doctor short since we lost Jonathan. I've interviewed a few but haven't found anyone suitable. Now, in your case you've done hospital work and have also done some GP training with a view to branching into it. Naturally I'd want to know all about what you've done and where and for how long.'

'But suppose you didn't think I was suitable when you'd interviewed me?'

'Then it really would be milking the cows at five o'clock in the morning,' he told her laughingly.

'You think I'm not coping, don't you?' she said flatly, 'after finding this place a shambles yesterday.'

'The only thing I'm thinking is that you need some help as anyone caring for a baby on their own does. So what about it?'

'It's a crazy idea,' she protested. 'You're still a complete stranger. I know nothing about you. It wouldn't be fair to Jonathan to take him to live with someone I don't know.'

'I'm the village doctor...not the local rapist. But if you have doubts, why not come for a short stay and make your decision after that? Pack your bags in the morning and come for a week. That way you're not committing yourself to anything that you might regret.'

'All right,' she said slowly, and knew that she *was* curious about this man and his background, and the village that he spoke of so fondly. In another situation she might find the thought of rural living uneventful, but the idea of a restful week with a willing helper was too appealing to turn down.

'Good,' he said, 'and am I going to get a peep at my nephew before I drive back to Derbyshire tonight?'

'He's due for his last bottle of the day in a moment. You can give it to him if you like,' she said, feeling that she must make amends for her earlier ungraciousness.

Drew's face lit up.

'Wonderful. Getting to know Jonathan is something I never expected to have the pleasure of.'

CHAPTER TWO

As ANDRINA drove into the place that Drew had spoken of with such fondness the previous day, she understood where his love of the village came from.

Limestone cottages with neat gardens snuggled up to solid oak doors and there were shops on the main street of the kind she hadn't seen in years, each with its own individuality, scorning the anonymity of the supermarket.

Behind them, rising majestically towards the heavens, were the Pennines, the peaks described as the backbone of England. Today, beneath the August sun, they were looking down in green benevolence on the place where Drew had his practice.

He'd told her it was at the end of the main street and, sure enough, there it was—another limestone building but larger and more imposing than some.

Jonathan had slept most of the way but now as she stopped the car outside the practice, he opened eyes that were the same deep blue as his uncle's and gazed around him.

'We're here, my precious one,' she told him, and wondered again if she'd taken leave of her senses in coming to the place where Drew wanted his nephew to grow up. Was he hoping that the village would cast its spell on her, too, and she would want to stay? Everything was moving too fast. She'd only known him two days and he was taking over her life.

Lifting Jonathan out of his car seat, she stood with him in her arms looking around her. The man who'd persuaded her to come here had been right about one thing, she thought, the air smelt fresh and unpolluted.

The inside of the village practice was bright and attractive with pale yellow walls, a dark honey-coloured carpet, chairs and an occasional table to match.

Andrina hid a smile. Not twenty years behind the times, by any means, but, then, she'd met the man and should have known it wouldn't be. He gave off an air of style and efficiency himself, so it was to be expected that everything connected with him would be the same.

As she gazed around her the smile faded. Jodie had worked here, she thought, with the young doctor who had given her a child. Now they were gone and instead *she* was here with their child. Maybe this *was* where Jonathan should be, but not without her. Never that.

Two receptionists were in view behind a nearby counter, filing. The elder of them stopped what she was doing and asked, 'Can I help you?'

'I'm here to see Dr Curtis,' Andrina told her.

Bright, inquisitive eyes were taking stock of her.

'Morning surgery is finished, I'm afraid,' she said. 'Did you have an appointment?'

'Not exactly, but he *is* expecting me.'

'I see. Well, the doctor is out on his home visits, but will be back shortly if you'd like to wait. Is it the baby that isn't well?'

'No, he's fine. It's a personal matter I'm here about.'

At that moment the door opened and Drew came striding in, loosening his tie and shedding his jacket as he did so. When he saw her sitting there with the baby in her arms, his face lit up.

'Andrina! So you made it.'

His pleasure at seeing her was infectious and in spite of her doubts and deliberations she smiled back.

'Like you, I try not to say things I don't mean, and I *did* say I would come.'

The receptionist was tuning in to what they were saying. Taking Jonathan from her, Drew walked across to the counter and said, 'This is my nephew. Marion, meet Jonathan Curtis, junior.'

'Really!' she exclaimed. 'You mean this is Jonathan and Jodie's child! Well, I'm blessed! So where is she? Has she come back to us?'

He shook his head.

'Jodie is dead. She was killed in a car crash and Andrina, her sister, has been looking after the baby.'

The woman behind the counter held up her hands in horror.

'Oh, dear! Poor girl! Poor baby!'

'Yes, indeed,' he agreed sombrely, 'but fortunately he has us, Andrina and myself. That's why she has come here.'

Marion demonstrated that she was kind as well as inquisitive.

'Well, you know I'll do anything to help, and the rest of the folk around here will rally round if you need them. Jonathan was one of us and we all liked Jodie.'

Andrina felt tears prick her eyes. Here was another stranger who had crossed her path and was showing compassion, but the feeling of everything moving too fast was still there.

Drew hadn't told the receptionist she was only here for a visit, that she'd come to get the feel of the place before making any big decisions, but courtesy demanded that she thank Marion for her kind offer so she said, 'It's very kind of you to say you'll help us should we need it, but Jonathan and I may not be staying very long.'

'Oh, I see,' she said disappointedly. 'So I'm not going to get the chance for a cuddle.'

Drew's smile had disappeared while Andrina had been explaining that her stay might be short, but it was back again as he said, 'Yes, you will, Marion. Trust me. And now I'm taking Andrina and the baby to my place. James will take the late surgery for me. He's capable enough. Tell him to give me a call if anything crops up that he can't handle.'

As they went out to their cars he was still smiling and she eyed him questioningly.

'Marion has a heart of gold, but she is something of a busybody,' he said. 'She'll be on the village grapevine already, spreading the news, so don't be surprised if everyone knows all about you when you meet them.'

'I'm not sure how I feel about that,' she said slowly. 'It's all too much, being lifted from obscurity to all this. And could we please get one thing clear? You told Marion that I *have* been looking after Jonathan, as if it was a thing of the past. Well, it isn't. Where he goes I go.'

'Why are you so doubtful about my motives?' he protested. 'I've told you that I have no intention of causing grief to either of you. Will you, please, believe me?'

'Yes, but if we came to live here, who would be in a minority? Me! From what Marion said the villagers would receive your brother's son with open arms, as you are doing. But what about me? I'm not prepared to be relegated to the sidelines.'

Drew was frowning.

'If that is how you feel, you will just have to trust me. I'm not used to being looked on with suspicion, but I suppose under the circumstances it is only natural. Perhaps you would have been happier if I'd run a mile from what I see as my responsibility. But this isn't getting us any nearer to settling you in at Whistler's Farm. It's about half a mile away, up on the hillside. If you follow my car, I'll lead the way.'

The part of the farmhouse that he had renovated was as tasteful and relaxingly furnished as the surgery, with the addition of a sort of toned-down elegance, and as Andrina looked around her she couldn't help but think that it would be hard to deny Jonathan the privilege of living in such a place.

Drew was clever, she thought. He'd seen her apartment, knew there was no comparison, and during the next few days would be unfolding before her the pleasures of village life, in the hope that she would succumb.

Andrina had unpacked their things in a spacious bedroom that was almost as big as the whole of her flat put together, and now she was seated on a kitchen stool holding Jonathan while Drew prepared a meal.

It was warm in the room with the afternoon sun on it and the heat from the oven, and she yawned.

He looked up from chopping vegetables and eyed her sympathetically.

'Does Jonathan wake up much in the night?' he asked.

'Yes. I'm afraid so. He has his last feed at about ten and usually lets me know he is hungry again around two. Why do you ask?'

'I suggest that once we've eaten you go and catch up on some sleep. I'll give him his late feed and see to him in the night.'

'That's a very tempting offer. I'll make up a couple of bottles before I go,' she told him.

'No need,' he said calmly. 'I *am* a doctor, you know. Just tell me the quantities and I'll do the rest.'

'You may be a doctor,' she told him, 'but you're not a father, are you? You mightn't hear him in the night.'

She saw him wince and wished she could stop being on the defensive. However, he didn't take her up on the comment, just pointed to the stairs when they'd eaten and said, 'Your bedroom has an *en suite* bathroom so when you're ready to head for sleep, feel free. Jonathan will be perfectly all right with me.'

Andrina woke up in the night in a panic. Unsure of where she was for a moment, she felt frantically around her in the darkness for the sides of Jonathan's cot. As her eyes became accustomed to the gloom it all came flooding back, and with the memory was the realisation that she'd left Jonathan in the care of a stranger. Drew may be his uncle, but he was a stranger as far as she and Jonathan were concerned.

Not waiting to put on a robe, she went out onto the landing dressed in just a long cotton nightdress, and as she hesitated saw a light on below. As she went down the stairs the clock in the hall said it was two a.m.

The door to the sitting room was open, and as she looked in she saw Drew feeding the baby his bottle. Clad in just a pair of boxer shorts, he was totally engrossed in what he was doing and as she stood watching Andrina couldn't help but be aware of his attractiveness.

His chest was broad and tanned, with golden body hair the same colour as that on his head. His hips were trim inside the smart cotton shorts and she thought wryly that she didn't feel the least bit shrivelled up inside, as Jodie had once teased she would become if she didn't get involved with a man soon.

Drew looked up suddenly and saw her standing there. There was a sort of satisfied contentment in his expression and in that moment she knew he was cut out to be a family man. That one day he would make some child a wonderful father. But she wasn't going to let Jonathan fill the slot just to satisfy his uncle's yearnings.

'No need to check on us,' he said softly. 'We're both fine. I took Jonathan's cot into my room so you wouldn't be disturbed. He woke up a few moments ago and made it clear that he was hungry.'

She nodded.

'I'm really looking forward to the time when he will go through the night.'

'It won't be long hopefully,' he said. 'When they reach a certain weight babies usually begin to sleep for longer periods.'

This is incredible, she was thinking. *I'm* here in my nightdress. The most attractive man I've met in ages is in his underwear, and all we can talk about is babies sleeping through the night. It was a sign of the times as far as she was concerned. What Drew was thinking she didn't know, but was about to find out.

'Go back to bed,' he told her. 'We'll be up shortly once the bottle is empty and Jonathan is winded.' And because it was too good an offer to refuse, she did so, curling up under the covers with peace of mind for the first time in weeks.

When she came down to breakfast the next morning Jonathan was lying in his pram, gazing around him contentedly, and Drew was standing by the kitchen table, dressed in a dark suit, eating a piece of toast.

As she observed the scene in some surprise he said, 'It's a suit and tie job again this morning. I have morning surgery at half past eight and house calls afterwards, but I'll call back here early this afternoon to make sure you're both all right. There are eggs and bacon in the oven and porridge simmering on the stove here. A nourishing breakfast is what you need

to complement a good night's sleep. *Did* you
sleep well?'

'Yes. Like a log.'

'Good. What do you think you'll do while
I'm out? Have a look around the village
maybe?'

She smiled. 'Yes, why not? It looked very
nice as I drove in, but I didn't get much chance
to look around while I was in the car. With
Jonathan in the pram, I can take a leisurely
stroll.'

'You won't be disappointed,' Drew said as
he picked up his bag and headed towards the
door, 'but remember what I said about Marion.
You'll receive some curious glances and will
find that people may want to stop and chat, so
be prepared.' And on that note he went.

It *would* be nice to have a proper look
around the village, she supposed as she cleared
away the breakfast things some time later.
She'd enjoyed the meal immensely, unable to
remember the last time someone had cooked
for her.

Maybe it was all part of the plan to make her want to stay, but as she'd eaten the good wholesome food it hadn't seemed to matter all that much.

She was feeling rested and less apprehensive this morning, and if she did have to cope with the curiosity her arrival had aroused she would have to put up with it.

She'd needed a change of scene badly—hadn't realised just how much until now. Ever since that dreadful night in July the only joy in her life had been the baby. But Drew seemed determined to broaden her horizons and so far he wasn't making a bad job of it.

Marion was waiting to pounce the moment Drew walked through the door of the surgery, and he took her into his consulting room so they wouldn't be overheard.

'I still can't believe it,' she said the moment the door was closed behind them. 'Jodie dead. That child an orphan and a strange woman is in charge of him. Who did you say she was?'

'Andrina Bell. Jodie's stepsister. She was sent for when the accident occurred and has been looking after him ever since. She came here yesterday at my invitation. I'm hoping the two of them will move in with me for a while.'

He gave a twisted smile. 'Unfortunately, she seems to doubt my motives. Andrina is very protective of the baby, which is not surprising as he was thrust upon her out of the blue and she's had to rearrange her life accordingly. All I want to do is help, but she seems to see me as a threat.'

'Yes, well, she will, won't she?' Marion said. 'You are the blood relative. She is only related by marriage.'

'That may well be, but my thoughts aren't running along those lines. At this moment all I want to do is help…if she'll let me.'

'How did you find her?'

'As you know, I'd been to see Jodie a couple of times in London to make sure she was all right physically and financially, but the last time I went her flat was empty. No one could tell me where she had gone. So I looked up her records here and went to look for the woman whose name was there as next of kin.'

'And so what *are* this Andrina's plans?' Marion wanted to know.

'I'm not sure. She isn't giving anything away at the moment, except the feeling that she is wary of me. We're going to have a chat when I get back from my rounds.'

'See if you can persuade her to stay. We'll all rally round.'

His smile flashed out. 'Great minds think alike, Marion. But getting down to the day's duties, how many are there waiting?'

'An average number, I'd say,' she told him. 'Young James has already started seeing some of the less urgent cases. That young fellow will be a godsend to somebody's practice one day.'

It was a fact that the trainee he'd taken on recently was a very capable twenty-one-year-old. And once he'd found someone to replace his brother, running the practice should be plain sailing. As it had been before Jodie Stewart had appeared and she and Jonathan had fallen in love. At that time there hadn't been a cloud in the sky. Never, ever had he expected it all to end as it had.

Drew and Jonathan had put the money their parents had left them into the practice and had worked together for five years until, shortly after he'd become engaged to Jodie, Jonathan had been diagnosed with leukaemia. The disease had been painful and relentless and their time together had been short-lived, but long enough for her to fall pregnant.

For the first time in her life Jodie had been made to look deeper than the surface of things and she hadn't been able to cope, especially as she'd been carrying Jonathan's child. She'd left the village, saying she couldn't bear to stay there any longer.

He'd begged her not to go. He'd told her that it was his nephew she was carrying and she must let him have an address or he would be worried sick about her. But she'd still gone. The only reassuring thing had been a promise to come back for the birth.

But in the end his brother's child had been born in the A and E department of a London hospital, and he'd known nothing about it until three days ago when he'd knocked on the door of a high-rise apartment in the Midlands.

His life had changed in that moment, just as Andrina's had on the night of Jodie's accident, and he knew that it would never be the same again. Not with an orphaned baby to consider, along with the hazel-eyed woman who was so fiercely protective of him.

As she looked in the window of a small grocer's shop called Bovey's, Andrina was amazed to see an assortment of cheeses that would have put a larger food store to shame. Inside she could see an elderly man in a spotless white apron serving a customer with butter from a big wooden tub. There was a large basket of free-range eggs on the counter beside him and the shelves behind were stocked with various jars of home-made preserves.

It was as if everything was conspiring to make her aware of the wholesomeness of the place, she thought wryly.

'Old Bovey's butter melts in the mouth,' a voice said from beside her, and when she turned an elderly man leaning on a stick was observing her with twinkly grey eyes.

'Does it really?' she said in a voice that matched her thoughts.

He'd gone over to the pram and was looking down at the baby as he said, 'I'm Frank Fairley and this, I take it, is young Jonathan's offspring. I can remember his father when he was this small.'

'Yes, this is Jonathan junior,' she told him, without elaboration.

The old man shook his head. 'It's been a sad affair all round. And now it's up to you and Dr Curtis, I take it.'

'Yes, something like that,' she said, anxious to be on her way.

'There's a lot of folk here who knew 'em both,' he said, 'and will do what they can to help. Just a matter of asking, that's all.'

Tears weren't far away again as Andrina listened to him. In those first weeks after she'd taken Jonathan home she would have given anything to hear someone say that. She'd never felt so alone in her life, and she was realising that if she'd been in this place during that time, it would have been different.

But now everything had changed. She'd met Drew and she wished that she knew what was really going on in his mind. What *his* plans and *his* needs were.

It was clear to see that he loved children. Anyone seeing him with Jonathan would know that. But why hadn't he got any of his own? He would be seen as a catch in any woman's book, yet that didn't appear to have taken him to the altar. From what she knew of him so far, he was as solitary as herself.

The old man touched his cap and tapped his way along the street towards the post office while Andrina followed at a slower pace. When she got there the postmistress was outside on the pavement, putting an advertisement into the big glass case on the wall nearby. She gave a shy smile into the pram, then shook her head.

'Poor wee mite, and what a lot of responsibility for you and the doctor,' she said. 'But it will be nice to see him grow up among us.'

Andrina was left with the feeling that Marion had indeed been busy.

Set back from the pavement at the end of the village was the local pub, the Grouse, and as it was midday Andrina wasn't surprised to see that it was the busiest place she'd seen yet, with customers spilling out onto the wooden tables and chairs outside.

It was all very idyllic on a warm summer morning, but what would it be like in winter? she wondered with her glance on the peaks towering above. Those green slopes would be bleak, with snow in the gullies. How would Drew describe his paradise in those months of the year?

If she became a GP in the practice she would have to drive up there to visit outlying patients. She was a town person, used to being where there was transport and gritted roads in bad weather.

You're just making excuses, she told her-self, and Drew will know it if you start going along those lines. She was passing the only garage that the place seemed to possess, and a man on the forecourt in country tweeds was observing her curiously.

He came across, blocking her path, and asked, 'Can this be the sprog that my friend Drew has taken under his wing? You fit the description of the stand-in mother.'

And what sort of a description was that? Andrina wondered. A tall brunette with a washed-out appearance? Yet she felt that his glance was on her rather than on the baby. He was tall and gangling with russet hair and freckles, and from the sound of it he was a friend of Drew.

'Yes, this is Drew's nephew,' she said qui-etly, 'and you are?'

'Eamon Dawlish. Owner of the garage. I've known Drew for a long time. He's a great guy, especially with waifs and strays.'

'Is that so?' she said stiffly. 'Maybe I should point out that this baby is not a waif and I have not strayed here. I was invited.'

He smiled back at her, unabashed.

'Sure thing. Remember, if you need any car repairs while you're here, this is the place to come.'

'Thanks. I'll bear that in mind,' she told him, and went on her way feeling somewhat ruffled.

There would be no long silences and infrequent rings of the doorbell in this place, she thought as she made her way back to the farm. There mightn't be much privacy either. But she'd had her fill of long hard slogs at the hospital and then falling into bed to be ready to drag herself out of it the next morning. And now that Jonathan was on the scene, coping with that sort of a job would be even harder.

She'd given him his lunchtime bottle, found some cheese in the fridge to make herself a sandwich, and was seated on a bench in the garden with the baby in her arms when Drew came striding up the path in the middle of the afternoon.

When he was level Andrina got to her feet.

'Have you eaten?'

'Yes,' he replied. 'Have you?'

'Mmm.'

'How was your tour of the village?'

'A mixture of things.'

'Such as?'

'Impressive, illuminating, irritating.'

'Oh, did someone say something to upset you?'

'Everyone was lovely…'

'Except?'

'The man who owns the garage came across and was rather patronising.'

Drew groaned. 'That would be Eamon. What did he say?'

'Just that you were into waifs and strays.'

'He's a good man but he can be a clown sometimes. Thinks he's God's gift to the female sex, for one thing.'

She ignored that.

'Is that how you see us?'

'What?'

'As charity cases?'

'No. Of course not!' he said abruptly. 'You've got plenty of get up and go of your own without needing anyone's charity. What do I have to do to convince you that I have no hidden agenda?'

'I'm sorry for being so prickly,' she said contritely. 'Do, please, forgive me. It's just that I'm very sensitive about anything concerning Jonathan and me. Apart from having my feathers ruffled by your friend, everything else is lovely. I can understand why you love this place so much. But at the risk of being seen to be difficult again, what is it like in winter? The thought of visiting patients amongst the peaks in blizzards is a bit nerve-racking.'

'You'd cope,' he said confidently. 'And if there *was* any danger, I would never put you at risk in any way.'

His face had been sober ever since she'd mentioned Eamon, but it was lightening as he said, 'So you *are* considering my suggestion, then?'

'It was just a passing thought. And in any case, you haven't checked me out yet.'

'Let's discuss it tonight. You can tell me all about yourself and I'll tell you what will be involved.'

'All right,' she agreed, 'but you have to give me time, Drew.'

'Of course,' he agreed, and wanted to add, But don't take too long. I want you both under my roof. But he thought better of it. If he appeared too eager she would start having doubts about his motives again.

Reassured by his answer, she smiled, and as always it transformed her face, made the pale skin covering fine bone structure glow and the eyes that had been wary and unwelcoming when he'd first appeared on the scene luminous.

'I have the afternoon surgery to do yet,' he said, 'but once that is over the rest of the day is ours.'

'I'll start the meal if you like,' she offered. 'So that it will be ready when you come home.'

'That would be great. There are steaks in the fridge and fresh vegetables and ice cream for afterwards. If that's all right with you.'

'Yes, it will be fine. I bought a bottle of wine in the village so we'll open that, shall we?'

'Yes, why not?' he agreed. He looked down at the baby in her arms. 'And what about our child. Has he been good?'

'Yes, not a murmur. I think that you're both in a conspiracy to make me stay.'

Her colour had risen. *Our* child, he'd said. She knew it was only a figure of speech, but it made her feel all trembly inside. One day he would say that to some lucky woman and mean it in the true sense.

That evening, after Jonathan had been settled, they talked about all sorts of things but mainly about the job at the practice. Drew asked questions and was impressed with Andrina's answers.

Finally he said, 'The fact that you've done GP training is ideal, and that you seem to have worked on most of the wards in the hospital where you were employed is also a great advantage. If you came to live here you would have a lot of benefits. A more relaxed lifestyle in the countryside, a job that, though demanding, wouldn't be quite so stressful as the one you'd left, and someone to share the responsibility of looking after Jonathan.

'Obviously we would both be free agents in our personal lives and if either of us ever wanted to settle down with someone we met, we would have to have a rethink.'

He was observing her questioningly. 'I'm taking it that there isn't anyone in your life at the moment or you would have said so.'

'That's correct,' she informed him, feeling that the admission made her appear even more unprepossessing.

'During these first few months of his life I think Jonathan needs us both,' he continued, without any reference to what she'd just said. 'What do you say, Andrina?'

'What I have to say is this,' she said levelly. 'Do you really want me as part of the practice or is it the waifs and strays thing? Are you going to find me a niche so that you can have Jonathan here?'

'Nothing of the kind. You joining the practice would be the ideal solution. You would be independent of me, for one thing. It's quite clear that you don't like taking favours from anyone.

'I think I should point out that the surgery is one of the focal points of the village. The other being the Grouse.' He laughed. 'They go in there to drink and then come across to us to have their livers checked.'

He became serious again. 'So is it a deal, Andrina? Are we going to team up?'

'I think so,' she told him, 'but I've only been here a day. Let me sleep on it.'

She was well aware that he was offering her the solution to all her problems, yet would it create a new set that would be even harder to deal with? She wished she knew.

But the long-term future was something she could face up to when the time came. It was the present that had been her nightmare. Now there was light at the end of the tunnel. She was being offered the position of a country GP. Drew was impressed with her track record, and if she agreed to his proposal, Jonathan was going to be brought up in the place where his father and uncle had spent their youth.

Over breakfast the next morning she told him, 'I've made a decision, Drew. I'm going to accept your offer, as long as I'm allowed to share household expenses with you, and you tell me straight if ever you want to end the arrangement for any reason. I promise to do the same.'

He smiled his delight across the table.

'Agreed,' he said. 'I'll set up a contract about your employment at the surgery, and start making one of the small bedrooms into a nursery for Jonathan. What will you do about your place?'

'Put it up for sale. Box-like though they are, there's a big demand for apartments.'

CHAPTER THREE

THE week that followed was hectic, with Andrina taking Jonathan back to Gloucestershire with her while she sorted out her affairs at that end and Drew working hard on the nursery.

She sent in her resignation to the hospital and thought a few times that it was perhaps as well that she was busy, otherwise she might have been wondering if she was doing the right thing by taking what seemed like the easy way out.

But there was another reason for what she was doing, and it concerned Drew himself. She was now ready to believe him when he said that his only desire was to help, and it wasn't just because he was offering her a place in his home and his practice. Drew was the only man she'd been really aware of in a long time and she wanted to get to know him better.

It was an amazing thing that someone like him didn't appear to be in any kind of relationship. And apart from his dead brother, he hadn't mentioned any other family, so it would seem that he was, like her, pretty much on his own.

The assumption that Drew had no one else in his life lasted until the Sunday night at the end of a busy week. Andrina and the baby had now moved in with him, and in the nursery all that remained to be done was to hang blue curtains with teddy bears on them at the windows.

'This room is lovely,' she told Drew. 'The nursery at my place was a corner of the lounge.'

He grinned across at her, pleased that she was happy, and said, 'Nothing but the best for Jonathan, Andrina.'

She nodded, thinking that he was so easy about everything, so reasonable. He would make a wonderful father for children of his own one day. For a crazy moment she wondered what it would be like if Jonathan was theirs. Life would be so much simpler if they weren't just stand-in parents.

'Anyone at home?' a voice called up the stairs at that moment, and for the first time since she'd met him she saw Drew with a grimace on his face. But it was only for a moment as he went onto the landing and called down to the person below. 'Tania! What are *you* doing here?'

As a head of glossy dark hair appeared over the bannister Andrina felt herself tensing. She hadn't a clue who the visitor was but she sensed that she meant something to Drew.

The body that went with the head became visible and she noted that it wasn't short on curves. But if *she* was surprised at the interruption, Tania was dumbstruck as she took in the blue and white nursery. Then her gaze swivelled to Andrina and it was as if a chill wind had suddenly sprung up.

'What on earth is going on?' she asked Drew, who was carrying on hanging the curtains. 'Why do you need a nursery?'

At that moment she had her answer. Jonathan, who'd been asleep downstairs, had woken up and was exercising his lungs.

'A baby!' she exclaimed. 'You've got a baby in the house.' She turned to Andrina. 'Whose is it? Yours?'

'Yes, in a manner of speaking,' she said coolly. 'Although his birth mother was Jodie Stewart.'

A smile spread over a face that was a mixture of petulance and dark allure.

'And where is she?'

'Jodie is dead, Tania,' Drew said in a low voice.

'Oh! Good grief! How? What happened?'

'She was killed in a car crash.'

'Really! When?'

'Just over a month ago.'

'Hmm. Right.'

She wasn't exactly devastated, Andrina thought, and wasn't surprised when Drew changed the subject.

'How have you enjoyed your holiday?' he asked.

'It was fabulous,' she gushed. 'I went with a great crowd, but it wasn't the same without you. See, that's how much I missed you.' She held out her left hand and wiggled her fingers under his nose.

'Take the ring off, Tania,' he said coldly. 'We've gone into all that. It's over.'

She pouted at him with full red lips.

'You can't forgive me, can you? In spite of all the times I've said I'm sorry.'

'No, I can't, but this isn't the place to be arguing. I'm sure Andrina doesn't want to hear us…and, by the way, she and the baby are going to be living here in future.'

'What? Why, for goodness' sake?'

'Because little Jonathan needs someone to feed him, bath him and change his nappies. But you wouldn't know about those sorts of things, would you?'

'You're doing this out of spite, aren't you?' she snarled.

'No,' he told her with his calm intact. 'I'm doing it to fulfil a need, his and mine, and now, if you don't mind, we have things to do.'

'My luggage is downstairs,' she told him. 'I paid off the taxi. Are you going to run me home?'

'Yes, if you want me to, but I will be coming straight back.'

'So you're not going to call in to see my parents.'

'No, I'm not.' He turned to Andrina. 'I won't be long, and when I get back I'll give Jonathan his bottle.'

'Whew!' Andrina breathed when they'd gone. So much for the good doctor having no women in his life. Who was the overpowering Tania? Someone who thought she had a claim to him, it would seem, though Drew hadn't fallen over himself to be friendly. But he *had* taken her home and, though he'd told her he wasn't stopping, it appeared that he was on visiting terms with her parents.

And the ring business. What had that been about? From where she'd been standing, she couldn't see what sort of a ring it was, but Drew had understood what the gesture meant.

He was back within minutes and came upstairs with Jonathan in his arms. Andrina knew immediately that he wasn't going to disclose anything about the unexpected visitor and she certainly wasn't going to ask. He didn't owe her any explanations. She was there for one reason only—because of Jonathan.

They'd arranged that Andrina would start at the practice in a week's time, to give her the chance to get settled in at the farm first, and as the days went by she found herself slotting into village life with a new zest.

It was heaven to be away from the incessant grind of traffic and the disturbances created by people in other apartments. Also, the air was like wine, especially first thing in the morning.

She was enjoying having a neighbouring farmer deliver full cream milk to the doorstep each day, instead of having to buy it in plastic containers from a supermarket shelf.

Drew was easy to live with. He gave her space and yet was there the moment she needed his help. And she imagined that

Jonathan didn't cry as much since they'd moved. Maybe he sensed that *she* was calmer.

There were *some* awkward moments in those first few days, which was to be expected. They came mostly in the evenings when Jonathan was asleep and the chores of the day were done. It was then that she realised how little she and Drew knew about each other.

They were strangers and moving in with someone she barely knew would have been the last thing she'd have considered in normal circumstances. But the situation wasn't normal—anything but. It had taken a parentless baby to make her do what she'd done, and only time would tell if it was a mistake.

After the first couple of evenings spent making polite conversation, Drew said, 'I'm going to carry on with what I used to do before you came, unless you have some plans of your own.'

Andrina shook her head. She'd no urge to venture into the night life of the village which was mostly centred around the Grouse, but had thought that might be where Drew was intending making for.

When he appeared moments later in old dungarees and a hard hat, she found herself laughing.

'What's the joke?' he asked.

'I was expecting you to be off to the pub.'

He smiled back. 'No such thing. I'm going to knock down the wall between what was the old dairy and the pantry in the derelict half of the house. I'll be well away from Jonathan's room so shouldn't disturb him.'

When he'd gone Andrina sat deep in thought. There'd been no mention of Tania since that night when she'd come calling, and she couldn't help but be curious. She must live nearby if the length of time it had taken him to drive her home was anything to go by. And yet they'd seen nothing of her since, but that didn't take away the feeling that she hadn't seen the last of her. Remembering her dark beauty made Andrina feel positively anaemic.

On very short acquaintance she would class Tania as superficial, and there was nothing like that about Drew. He was the most uncomplicated, unselfish man she'd ever met.

She had a feeling that he was finding *her* hard going, which was understandable if he mixed with women like Tania, and tonight it would seem that he couldn't stick another evening of trivialities and had used the renovations as an escape.

Perhaps he was already regretting his impulsive offers of a home and a place in the practice, realising that he was lumbered with her for the foreseeable future and was wishing he wasn't.

There was nothing like that in his attitude towards his nephew, though. He adored him. He went straight to wherever the baby was when he came in at the end of the day and would bathe him, feed him and wind him with an expertise that made Andrina feel clumsy and fumbling.

'Why didn't you offer to just have Jonathan?' she asked when he came in at suppertime.

He was hot, grimy...and puzzled by the question.

'What do you mean?'

'You didn't have to have me as part of the package. You could have hired a nanny.'

'What has brought this on?' he asked as he peeled off the dusty dungarees. 'Are you not happy here?'

'Yes, of course I am. Everything is wonderful. But, like I say, you didn't have to take me under your wing as well as the baby.'

'Is all this because you want out?' he said with a frown. 'That now I'm on the scene you'd like to bow out gracefully? Do you feel that you've done your bit?'

Andrina could feel her cheeks burning. She'd said what she had because she sensed that she was there on sufferance due to his generosity of spirit, and she didn't want charity.

'You've got it all wrong,' she said quietly. 'I asked you the question because I feel that you find me a liability. That I'm boring and under your feet.'

He smiled through the grime.

'Is all this because I went to do some work outside? Because if it is, my thoughts must have been similar to yours. I felt that you must be wishing you hadn't come. That *you* were bored. And if you *had* been thinking along the lines, I wouldn't have blamed you. We're a crazy pair, aren't we?'

'Yes,' she agreed, her face softening. 'Maybe in future we shouldn't keep our thoughts so much to ourselves.'

'Agreed. And now, if you'll promise not to have any more negative vibes while I'm gone, I'm going to take a shower, and then maybe we could watch the late night movie.'

She was happy now. Drew had the knack of simplifying all problems. Maybe in time she might be able to learn to do the same.

That hope was to be short-lived. Andrina was getting Jonathan ready to go out the following morning when, as if her thoughts of the night before had transferred themselves, she heard a key turn in the lock. Then the front door swung back and Tania came striding in.

Andrina's first thought was, Oh, dear! And the second that the woman must have a key to the farmhouse. Any further observations didn't get the chance to surface as the unexpected caller was asking coldly, 'Is Drew here?'

'No. He'll be in the middle of morning surgery,' Andrina told her, thinking that she shouldn't need to be told that. 'Is there anything *I* can do?'

The ring she'd been flaunting on the previous occasion was clearly visible at that moment, and it was the plain gold band of matrimony. Surely she wasn't married to someone else and involved with Drew.

Tania laughed. It was a scornful, metallic sort of sound that grated on the ear.

'Yes, there *is* something you can do. You can tell me what you are doing here. Taking advantage of Drew's good nature from the looks of it.'

'I would have thought it was obvious,' Andrina told her, still keeping cool. She looked down into the pram. 'We have an orphaned baby here. Drew and I are his only living relatives and my connection is by marriage rather than blood. When Jodie died I had to take care of him. It was difficult. I had my own life sorted, hadn't a clue about looking after babies and was totally horrified at the prospect.

'Drew came to my place looking for Jodie and was devastated when he found out what had happened to her. It prompted him to ask me to move in here with Jonathan so that he could share the responsibility of looking after him. Does that satisfy you? Even though it's none of your business.'

'Oh! So you're not as meek and mild as you look,' Tania said mockingly. 'And is that the only reason you're here? It's not because you think his generosity might extend to taking you off the shelf, as I don't see any wedding ring on *your* finger.'

This is awful, Andrina was thinking. She was rowing with a woman she hardly knew. But the comment about her being on the shelf had stung. Did she really appear so frumpish?

The ordeal was coming to an end, or so it seemed.

'I'll call in at the surgery, then,' Tania was saying. And unable to resist a parting shot, she added, 'It's the talk of the village, what is going on here.'

'I don't see why!' Andrina told her, stung again by what she was inferring. 'Those villagers that I've met so far have been most supportive. People are stunned to know that Jodie is dead and have offered to do anything they can to help. So maybe you've been letting your imagination run away with you. Perhaps you would like to see Drew's reputation soiled.'

It actually seemed as if Tania had run out of words as she turned on her heel and went stalking off down the drive.

Andrina closed the door behind her and then sat down on the bottom stair and wept for them all. Jodie, Drew's brother, their son, herself and, taking poetic licence, Drew, who was being pursued by a shrew.

Surely there had to be some joy in it somewhere, and, of course, there was. She'd met a man who was far more willing to have his life turned upside down than she had been. Further than that she wasn't going to think. Not with Tania hovering, her new job at the practice and the needs of the child in the pram.

When Drew came home late that afternoon he said, 'I believe you had Tania round here this morning.'

Andrina nodded, having decided that she would be careful what she said. He could easily accuse her of interfering in his life if she wasn't careful.

He sighed. 'The last thing I need is her interrupting morning surgery, but she's always been a law unto herself and nothing changes. I'd just had to tell Mrs D'Arcy from the old manorhouse that tests have shown she has breast cancer, and had the butcher waiting anxiously to know if his blood pressure had come down from last week's dangerous level, when Tania appeared, going on about unimportant matters such as if I was going to the hunt ball.'

'And are you?'

'I really don't know,' he said, as his smile flashed out. 'Tania thinks she can charm the birds out of the trees, but some birds prefer to stay on their perches. What did she have to say when she was here?'

'Quite a lot. She wanted to know what I was doing in your house. And said that we are the subject of gossip in the village.'

'And what did you say?'

'I put her right on both counts. I explained that I was here from necessity and no other reason, and that so far I'd found everyone most pleasant and concerned about Jonathan, rather than tittle-tattling about us.'

'Good for you,' he said easily, yet she sensed withdrawal in him and wasn't sure from where it came.

'Tania doesn't know what ails her at the moment,' he went on to say. 'As the only child of wealthy parents she's been thoroughly spoilt, and since she found that I'm not ready to dance to her tune any more she isn't very happy.'

'Did you know that she has a key?'

'No, I didn't, but I'm not surprised. It's all part of her not wanting to let go.'

'What happened between you?'

It was out. The question she'd been longing to ask since that night when Tania had walked in on them in the nursery.

Drew wasn't smiling now. His face was devoid of all expression, as if a shutter had come down over it.

'She's my ex-wife. We were divorced last year. It was about *my* love of children and *her* lack of it,' he said. 'She was pregnant and never told me. Instead, she went and had an abortion without my knowledge. I only discovered it by accident when I heard her talking to a friend on the phone. I almost lost my faith in human nature.'

'How awful for you,' Andrina breathed.

Now she understood why he'd been so anxious to help with Jonathan. If his own child had been lost to him, he could at least cherish his brother's.

He was waiting for her to say something else but it was as if she'd been struck dumb.

'You asked, Andrina,' he said, 'and I've told you. Surely you have something to say.'

'Yes, I have one thing,' she said, finding her voice.

'And what's that?'

'She didn't deserve you.'

That almost brought the smile back.

'I don't know about that. Maybe I was too trusting…or stupid perhaps. We still speak to each other, as you will have realised, but as far as I'm concerned that's it. If Tania wants a reconciliation she is in for a disappointment. But I'm afraid that's her way. When she has something she doesn't want it, but when she can't have it she won't rest until she's got it.'

It was the Monday morning of Andrina's second week in the village and she was due to present herself at the practice. They'd discussed how they were going to look after Jonathan while they were both employed there and come up with the idea that in the mornings they would take him with them. There were enough staff to keep an eye on him and give him a cuddle if he was fretful.

Then in the early afternoon Andrina would take him home while Drew and James did the calls, and with the late afternoon surgery they would take it in turns.

It was a strange feeling, being introduced to the staff. Andrina was immediately conscious of the difference between general practice and hospital care.

This was a more intimate, friendly set-up. A small group of people performing their different functions in health care in a rural community, with just as much enthusiasm and expertise as those employed in a big hospital.

James was a tall, serious-looking young man, but he gave her a friendly smile when they shook hands. Joanne and Isabel, the two practice nurses, were brisk and efficient mothers of schoolage children, and the other receptionist working alongside Marion was a quiet young woman in her twenties called Rachel.

As Andrina took her seat behind the desk in the consulting room that had belonged to

Drew's brother, she had the strangest feeling, as if there were other presences in the room. It was almost as if she could hear Jodie saying, Well done, 'Drina. You've come out of your shell at last.

But *was* becoming a country GP coming out of her shell? It wasn't what she'd intended. But she had an incentive. Two, to be exact. A better life for Jonathan, and the chance to live and work with Drew Curtis. Only time would tell if she was cut out for either thing, and on that thought she rang for her first patient.

It was a dubious elderly woman called Ellen Battersby and Andrina was greeted with, 'I usually see Dr Curtis. Why has he passed me on to you? He understands me.'

'I'm sure that he does, Mrs Battersby,' Andrina said with a smile. 'Maybe when I've been here a bit longer you'll think that about me, too. But if you don't let me treat you it isn't going to happen, is it? So why not tell me what's wrong?'

'It's me eyes. I've got cataracts, and as well as that I keep having these flashes.'

'Do you mean black floaters?'

'No. I mean lights that would put the Blackpool illuminations to shame.'

'I'm going to examine your eyes, Mrs Battersby,' Andrina told her, 'but really you need to see an eye specialist. In the average doctor's surgery we don't carry the equipment that they have, but let's have a look.'

An examination with an ophthalmoscope didn't reveal anything, but Andrina wasn't happy with the patient's description of the flashing lights that she was seeing.

'I'm going to send you to hospital,' she told her. 'I want your retinas checked. What you've been experiencing sounds to me like a vitreous detachment.'

'And what might that be?' Mrs Battersby wanted to know.

'It can happen to any of us as we get older. Inside the eyeball is a soft mushy pulp when we are young, but it becomes less moist with age and as it gets drier sometimes a portion of it detaches itself and brings the retina with it.

'I don't think it has done in your case, but I want it checked out. If you ever see what is like a dark curtain coming down over your vision, that is a detached retina and you must get it seen to immediately, or you could go blind. I'm going to ring the eye clinic at the hospital now. Do you have someone who can drive you there?'

'No.'

'All right. I'll ask for an ambulance to be sent. If you'd like to take a seat in the waiting room, one of the nurses will take care of you until it arrives.'

As Ellen Battersby got to her feet she smiled for the first time. 'You'll do for me,' she said with grudging approval and stomped out.

She was followed by a mother with a young girl who'd fallen onto her wrist the previous day while playing netball at school and now it was painful and swollen.

'Do you think it's broken, Doctor?' the anxious mother asked.

'I don't know,' Andrina told her. 'An X-ray will be needed to tell us that. It's possible that it is just a very bad sprain, but I'm going to have to send you to A and E to make sure.'

The mother groaned. 'That's half the day gone, then. We've never been dealt with quickly in one of those places yet.' After that gloomy prediction they went, the girl quite enjoying the attention and the thought of missing school, and the mother not so pleased.

Marion came in between patients in the middle of the morning with a coffee, and before Andrina could ask about Jonathan she chirped, 'The staff are all waiting for a chance to pick up the baby, but he's being as good as gold. I think he likes his new surroundings.'

'He certainly seems more settled since we came to live here,' Andrina agreed.

They were both feeling more settled, she thought. In fact, she had never felt more settled in her life and had to keep telling herself that he wouldn't be a baby for long and then what would happen? They couldn't stay in Drew's house for ever.

It was leaping ahead somewhat, crossing her bridges before she'd got to them. She hadn't been living in this place more than a couple of weeks and already she was looking for difficulties. While Drew, with his own brand of magic, was intent on ironing them out.

'So you're the new doctor,' a burly fellow said when she looked up some moments later after filling in the notes of the previous patient.

'Yes, I'm Andrina Bell,' she told him, sensing that he was uncomfortable for some reason, 'and I'm looking forward to getting to know everyone.'

'My name's Tom Blair,' he said. 'I have the Home Farm at the end of the village. I asked to see Drew, but Marion said he's booked up for the next few days. I never know when to believe her, though. If that one can make me hot under the collar, she will.'

So this was another of the regulars who didn't like change, Andrina thought, but his next comment did explain why.

He shuffled about on the chair for a moment and then said, 'I've got an embarrassing problem.'

'Tell me about it,' she said calmly. 'I've worked on Men's Surgical in a big hospital quite a few times and there isn't much that I haven't seen.'

Still uncomfortable, he cleared his throat and said, 'I've got a rash.'

'Where?'

'Around my…you know.'

'Your genitals.'

'Yes… I'm sore and itching all the time.'

'Take your trousers off, then, Mr Blair, and we'll have a look.'

He hadn't exaggerated. The whole area was swollen and the skin was bright red and blistered.

'Is it possible that you might have a sexually transmitted disease? That you've had unprotected sex?'

He gave a dry laugh.

'I haven't been around a woman for the last ten years. I'm a widower. Wouldn't be for long if that Marion Meadows had her way, mind you. Naw, I use a lot of pesticides and I'm wondering if it's from one of them. If I forgot to wash my hands when I'd been to the toilet. Though I always wear gloves and even then I don't handle it direct.'

'You might have the answer,' she told him. 'I'm going to give you some cream which should bring relief pretty quickly. If it doesn't, we'll send you to the hospital, as pesticides and suchlike have some quite deadly chemicals in them.'

When he'd gone, looking less hot and bothered than when he'd walked into her consulting room, Andrina sat back in her chair and allowed herself a moment's amusement.

So Marion had her eye on the suffering farmer, she thought. She'd bet Marion could be a determined woman and remembering the ex-Mrs Curtis, there were a few of them about.

But on a more serious note, it *was* a nasty rash that he'd got and he was probably right about its origin. She would watch with interest to see if he came back.

Andrina was in Reception, cuddling Jonathan, when Drew came out of his room after seeing off his last patient. His eyes lit up.

'So how's it gone?' he asked.

'I enjoyed it. It was interesting. Mind you, I had to win over a couple of patients who would much rather have seen you.'

He nodded. 'I suppose that is only to be expected at first. Some of the locals are very set in their ways, but they'll adjust.'

He held out his arms and took the baby from her. As Drew looked down at Jonathan he said, 'And this little one has behaved himself, I hear.'

'Mmm,' she said. 'We can count day one as a success.'

His glance had moved to her. She wasn't to know it but he was rejoicing to see her happy. He felt more confident about everything when Andrina sparkled like she was doing now. There hadn't been much joy in her when they'd first met, understandably so, but now the clouds were lifting and for the present he was happy for it to be so.

The only thorn in his side at the moment was Tania. He had to admire her cheek. She'd betrayed him without a second thought, considering only her own needs. It was true what he'd told Andrina. When he'd discovered that she'd aborted their child he'd been devastated.

If there'd been something wrong with the foetus, or Tania had had a health problem that would have made pregnancy dangerous, he would have understood. He was a doctor, for heaven's sake. But to do it behind his back, because she hadn't wanted to spoil her figure and have the inconvenience of carrying the child for nine months, had torn him apart. And yet in his darkest moments he'd acknowledged that he wouldn't have wanted a child to come into the world with a mother like that.

When he'd married her she'd been fun. She'd brought excitement to the marriage, but that had been about all, he'd soon found. Tania was vain and selfish, with a sort of built-in arrogance that had shown itself in her behaviour when she'd found she'd been pregnant.

The arrogance was still there in the way she wouldn't accept that they were finished. In anyone else it would be humiliating, but not with Tania. She probably thought that he would give in eventually, unable to resist her.

When he'd met a woman who was the exact opposite to his ex-wife, in that she'd unselfishly turned her life round to care for someone else's child, and was physically more of a fresh garden flower than a hothouse bloom like Tania, he'd realised more than ever what a mistake his marriage had been.

'So you are going to take Jonathan home for lunch, then,' he said. 'James and I will get started on the house calls. With luck, it won't take too long.'

He wanted to be back with them. Not just with Jonathan but Andrina, too. After Tania's moods and machinations she was good to come home to.

As Andrina drove back to the farm her heart was light. With each passing day she was becoming more certain that she'd made the right decision. She had brought Jonathan to live with a man who, though he wasn't his father, was as near to one as he would ever get, and deep down in her heart she knew that she couldn't have denied either of them the chance to get to know the other.

'I've been thinking,' Drew said when he arrived home later. 'We should arrange a christening. When do you think it should be?'

Andrina's face had clouded. The thought had been in her mind, too, but the images that it brought up had been upsetting. Christenings were usually joyful affairs where thanks were given for the birth of the child, and the parents and godparents made suitable vows.

There would be nothing joyful about this one, with both parents gone, and who could they ask to be godparents?

'I have thought about it myself,' she said slowly, 'but couldn't face the idea.'

'I'm happy to arrange it. Would you like me to?'

'Yes. All right. Who will you ask to be godparents?'

'Good question. It would probably have been us in different circumstances.'

'What about Marion?'

'Yes. I suppose so. It'll give *her* a buzz even if we find it hard going. And maybe I'll ask my friend Eamon, who has the garage. I know that he rubbed you up the wrong way that first day you were here, but he's really a decent sort and thoroughly reliable.'

'Whatever you say,' she agreed, and went to stand by Jonathan's pram as if to protect him from life's hurts. On this occasion he wouldn't know what it was all about, but there would be other times when he would be vulnerable.

CHAPTER FOUR

ON THE morning of the christening Andrina awoke to a typical autumn day. The sun was melting the sparkling frost of what had been a chilly night and the first falling leaves were scattered around the gardens that surrounded Whistler's Farm.

There was no sound coming from Drew's room and when she looked into the nursery Jonathan was only just beginning to stir, so for a little while she had time to herself.

With elbows resting on the wide window-sill in her bedroom, she could see the steeple of the church rising heavenwards, a reminder of the solemn service they would be taking part in later that morning. It had been three weeks since Drew had suggested it, and in that time they'd been waiting for the vicar to come back from holiday and lining up the god-parents.

Marion had been delighted when he'd asked her to be godmother, and Eamon, who she'd discovered was unmarried, had agreed to be godfather after he'd got over his initial surprise.

There was silence all around her and maybe because of it her thoughts were crystal clear. She had fallen in love with this place. It would break her heart if she ever had to leave it, yet it could happen. If Drew got back with Tania they wouldn't want a third person hanging around, and that could create problems. He wouldn't want to let Jonathan go and she, Andrina, wouldn't let that woman anywhere near Jodie's child, so it could all turn out to be very awkward.

But she was doing it again. Crossing her bridges before she got to them. If Drew ever went back to his selfish wife he would not be the man of integrity and sweet reason that she thought he was, but the human mind was a strange thing.

There were noises coming from the nursery now and she padded across to the cot. Big dark eyes looked up at her and suddenly the child lying there smiled. Not a windy movement of the face, but a toothless little beam of recognition, and her heart stood still. It was a moment of bonding. Another stepping stone in the new life that she'd been persuaded into.

Tenderness was spreading through her in a warm, cleansing tide in that sweet moment of communication. She'd loved Jonathan from the start, but the smile he had just bestowed on her had come from a person, not a worrying responsibility. Someone who was going to be part of her life for ever.

She bent and picked him up, holding him to her as if she would never let him go. Then the tears began to flow. Tears of happiness for a special moment on that day of all days.

'Andrina!' Drew's voice cried frantically from the doorway. 'What's wrong? What's happened?'

He was flinging himself across the room and when he saw the baby lying serenely in her arms he went limp with relief.

'What is it?' he wanted to know, his gaze switching to her tear-blotched face. 'You frightened the life out of me. I thought for a ghastly moment…' His voice trailed away and, choking back the tears, she finished the sentence for him.

'That we had a cot death or something like that? No, Drew, it's me. Jonathan smiled at me. Really smiled as if he knew me. It was wonderful.'

The panic had subsided and his face was softening in the rays of the early morning sun. He didn't offer to take the baby from her, as he might have done under normal circumstances. Instead, he put his arms around them both and with her head resting beneath his chin he said softly, 'Your face was one of the first he saw in this world and you've been looking down at him and watching over him ever since. You're so wonderful with him. So caring and meticulous about his welfare. In spite of his lack of parents, Jonathan is a fortunate child.'

With her head buried against Drew's chest, she could tell that he was smiling as he said, 'And he's a charmer like his father was.'

'And his uncle *is*,' she said in a muffled voice.

Drew put his finger under her chin and lifted her face to his.

'I don't know about that, but you're quite something yourself.'

'Me! Tania thinks I'm a frump,' she told him with a watery smile. 'She wanted to know if I was hoping that you would take pity on me and take me down off the shelf.'

He laughed low in his throat.

'Did she, now? If anyone is likely to end up alone, she'll be the one. Tania didn't care about her own child, let alone anyone else's, and as far as I'm concerned that says it all.'

He was still looking into her reddened eyes.

'It's fitting that today of all days Jonathan should capture your heart all over again. We have a big day before us, Andrina. The christening this morning, followed by lunch at the Grouse with the godparents. Then this evening

I'm going to take you out, just the two of us, to say thank you.'

She blinked.

'What for?'

'Being there for Jonathan…and me. You've cared for my precious nephew, filled the empty slot in the practice and brought some light into my life.'

'It's you that's brought light into *my* life,' she protested.

He was laughing as he held her close.

'We'll not argue about it. Suffice to say that we've both benefited.' And bending his head, he kissed her lightly on the brow.

Andrina became still. There had been little physical contact between them until now, but at the touch of his lips she was so aware of him that she barely heard Jonathan start to remind them that he wanted his breakfast.

She was drowning in Drew's blue gaze, longing for him to kiss her on the mouth. As if he read her mind she saw warmth kindle in the eyes looking into hers and held her breath.

But quite unaware that the magic of the morning was wrapping around those who loved him, the baby in her arms was getting restive. The faint wail was about to become a full-volume protest and relaxing his hold Drew said, 'Which would you rather do? Make the breakfast or feed the baby?'

'I don't mind,' she told him, still bemused by that moment of awareness and the promise of some time alone with him that evening, though she had a question to ask about that.

'Who's going to look after this young man tonight if we're dining out?'

'His godmother,' he said. 'She volunteered.'

The christening was to take place in the middle of the morning service, and as Andrina dressed the main participant in a smart white romper suit instead of the usual christening gown that Drew hadn't been keen on, she was trying not to let the thought of those who would be missing take the glow from the morning.

She'd often thought her stepsister shallow, but Jodie must have really loved Drew's brother—so much so that she couldn't bear to be in the place where they'd been together. If she'd stayed, as Drew had wanted her to, she might be alive today. But she'd gone away and then almost on the eve of the birth of her child tragedy had struck, which meant that today *she* and Drew would be standing in for the absent ones.

The church was full. The news that the doctors were having the orphaned baby christened had spread like wildfire and attracted the curious and the well-wishers.

On the way there Andrina had begun to feel apprehensive, but the moment she walked into the old stone church with Drew at her side she began to calm down. He was very serious. In a dark suit with a white shirt and a sober tie, she knew that he, too, was remembering those who were missing, and tears threatened again.

As if he guessed her thoughts he said in a low voice, 'No more tears, Andrina.' He looked down at the baby in her arms. 'For his sake.'

She nodded sombrely and as she did so the brim of the hat that she was wearing for the occasion tilted with the movement.

'I like the hat,' he whispered as his glance took in the pale cream straw she'd chosen to offset a smart black suit, and the dark moment passed, just as he had intended that it should.

They lunched at the Grouse, just the four of them and the baby, and now Marion had gone to her own pursuits until she was required that evening. But Eamon had come back to the farm with them and seemed in no hurry to depart.

His continued presence was explained when he took Andrina to one side and said. 'What sort of a relationship do you have with Drew?'

The man in question was strolling in the garden with Jonathan in his arms so wasn't present to hear what his friend had said, or her reply when it came, and Andrina was glad of it.

For one thing she wasn't sure how to answer. She was taken aback. Didn't know why he'd asked what he had. Except that she'd felt his glance on her a few times during the service.

'We have an arrangement whereby we are both equally responsible for Jonathan,' she told him. 'That is all. Drew adores him. When we first met we were both in a position where it would have been difficult to care for him alone and he suggested that I move in and at the same time fill the gap at the surgery.'

'And is it working?' Eamon wanted to know. 'Because in case you're not aware of it, Tania is still hovering. She'd like to get back to how it used to be.'

'Yes, I *do* know that,' she told him with feeling. 'And it puzzles me that Drew can tolerate having her around after what she did to him.'

'He might put up with her hanging around but Drew won't have her back,' his friend said. 'After the first anger and bitterness had died down he decided to get on with his life, and little Jonathan is just the kind of thing he needs to focus on.'

'Is all this leading up to something?' she asked curiously.

'Sort of. I'd like to spend some time with you. Would you come out with me on a date?'

'I see,' she said slowly. 'It's nice of you to ask, but I don't think so. I haven't a moment to spare. My time is fully occupied with the baby and my job at the practice.'

It wasn't strictly true, but she didn't want to offend the garage owner. He was a likable sort on further acquaintance, but he wasn't Drew and thereby lay his failure to attract her.

He didn't seem too put out by her refusal. 'Maybe another time, eh?'

Drew was back and observing them questioningly.

'Everything all right?' he wanted to know.

'Yes, sure,' Eamon said easily. 'I was asking Andrina for a date and wanted to make sure first that I wasn't muscling in on anything that might affect you. However, she tells me that she's too busy.'

'I see,' Drew said abruptly, and went back into the garden without a backward glance.

Andrina watched him go and wondered what he was thinking. Was he annoyed that his friend had asked her out in *his* house? And was he thinking that maybe she'd encouraged him? She hoped not. His good opinion mattered—a lot.

Eamon wasn't wasting any time, Drew thought edg ily as he strolled among the shrubs and flowers that he'd lovingly planted in the gardens of Whistler's Farm. But he was like that with women.

And what about Andrina? She'd told Eamon she was too busy. Was she feeling that she was too tied to their arrangement to make any out-side commitments? He hoped not. It was the last thing he would want—for her to feel she had to stay in all the time.

And yet, if he was honest, that was exactly what he wanted her to do. Stay with Jonathan and him.

What did she think of *him*? he wondered. Did she see him as an amiable wimp who was latching onto the lives of others because he hadn't got one of his own?

He'd been no wimp when he'd sorted Tania out. His hurt and anger had kept him going, but he had to admit that the arrival of Andrina and the baby had lifted him out of an all-time low.

It might seem a peculiar arrangement, the three of them all living together in the same house, but so far it was working. Jonathan was receiving the best of care, and both Andrina and himself were benefiting, too.

Well, *he* was anyway. He wasn't so sure about her. She seemed happy enough, but her face wasn't like an open book. Sometimes he caught an expression on it that made him uneasy. Made him feel that he didn't know her as well as he thought he did.

It was great having her with him at the surgery. She had a cool yet friendly approach that went down well with both staff and patients alike. For as long as he could remember, the doctors at the village practice had been men like himself and his brother. Now, according to Marion, the garrulous godmother, the women of the neighbourhood were delighted to be able to consult a woman doctor if they so wished.

Jim Sowerby, who had a pig farm down one of the many country lanes that were part of the parish, had been in to see him about a prostate problem, and when he'd been about to take his leave he'd said, 'My missus has been in to see the new doctor. She's had a lump in one of her bosoms for weeks and because she's a tidy size around those parts she was too embarrassed to come and see you. But the moment she heard there was a lady doctor here she made an appointment. We've both been worried sick about it and needn't have been. Dr Bell sent her for a mammogram and it turned out to be a non-malignant cyst.'

Drew had smiled.

'So *I'm* not going to be seeing your Janice any more, then.'

'Looks like it,' the weatherbeaten farmer had said. He'd shuffled awkwardly from one foot to the other. 'How's the little 'un doing?'

'Fine,' Drew had told him with the smile still there. 'Just fine.'

In fact, everything had been fine, and it had continued to be so until today.

Eamon asking Andrina out had brought him to earth with a jolt. All right, she'd refused the invitation, but it was making him think that there might be others coming along that she might want to accept and he didn't like the idea.

He'd been enjoying playing at happy families, having an attractive woman and a child in the house. Andrina didn't have the same kind of voluptuous attractions as his ex-wife, but heaven forbid that she should. He'd been down that road once and it hadn't been smooth.

Andrina was slender, fine boned, with bright intelligent eyes and a firm yet generous mouth. All Tania had to offer was her allure and she'd sacrificed their child for the sake of it.

He and Andrina looked after Jonathan together, ate together, did the chores together and even worked together. The only thing they didn't share, for obvious reasons, was a bed, because theirs was strictly a working partner-

ship and he wouldn't want it any other way...
would he?

The thought of having her beside him each
morning when he woke up was a pleasant one,
very pleasant indeed. Yet it had only entered
his mind since he'd discovered that Eamon
was sniffing around her. Or had it?

He'd once stood and looked down at her
while she'd been sleeping. Jonathan had been
grizzling in his cot beside her and he'd tiptoed
into the bedroom to pick him up so that she
wouldn't be disturbed.

She'd been beautiful in sleep, with one bare
arm flung across the pillows and the soft
mounds of her breasts rising and falling inside
a silk nightgown, but aware of the deal they'd
made he'd ignored a sudden rush of feeling
and taken the restless child into his own room.

Bringing his thoughts back to the present,
he looked and saw that Eamon was on the
point of leaving, and with his nephew still cuddled close to him he went to say goodbye.

When he'd gone Drew was aware that
Andrina was avoiding his glance and he

thought that the other man hadn't been very tactful, trying to date her and then mentioning her refusal in front of *him*.

She must sometimes think that privacy was in short supply in her life. Living with a man she hardly knew, caring for a child that wasn't hers, and then having the clown Eamon spouting off in front of her.

Impulsively he said, 'I hope you didn't say no to Eamon because of the situation here.'

What was that supposed to mean? Andrina wondered as the colour rose in her cheeks. Was Drew trying to tell her that she didn't always have to be glued to his side like a second rib? Or did he guess that she was beginning to have feelings for him and was warning her off by impressing on her that she was still a free agent, in spite of their domestic set-up? And that he didn't mind who she went out with?

It would appear so, as now he was saying, 'Don't forget, this is an equal partnership. We are both entitled to do what we like socially as long as one of us is there for Jonathan.'

'Yes, I *am* aware of that,' she told him stiffly. 'And if you want to get me from under your feet sometimes, you have only to say so. As to your friend Eamon, I hardly know him and don't particularly fancy him. Does that clarify matters?'

Drew was listening with head bent as he looked down at the baby, and she couldn't see his expression. If she had been able to, Andrina might have seen there a mixture of relief and annoyance.

Relief because she'd made her feelings about Eamon clear, and annoyance with himself for blundering into such a discussion and maybe making Andrina think he didn't care who she was attracted to as long as it wasn't him.

For the rest of the day there was constraint between them and it only lightened when Marion came round in the evening to babysit Jonathan. She adored him and was proud to be his godmother, and they felt that if there was one person they could safely leave the baby with it was Marion.

Andrina didn't have a lot of clothes. In her previous lifestyle there had been little time for socialising or shopping. The black suit she'd worn for the christening had been bought for a colleague's funeral and the cream straw hat a last-minute purchase months ago when she'd been invited to the wedding of one of the administrators at the hospital.

However, she did have an attractive dress that was semi-evening wear. She'd worn it at the hospital Christmas party and as she surveyed herself before going down to greet Marion she was hoping that for once Drew might see her as herself, instead of as Jonathan's aunt or his new colleague at the practice.

Made from soft, flame-coloured silk, the dress was calf-length and it clung to her hips and breasts like a second skin. She'd chosen to wear gold jewellery with it and high-heeled strappy evening shoes, and the effect was dazzling to say the least.

As she stood poised at the top of the stairs Drew was in the hallway below giving Marion her instructions about Jonathan's feeds and suchlike, but his voice trailed away when he saw her.

She held her breath. Was the transformation going to have the desired effect?

'So you're ready,' he said flatly, and turned away.

Marion made up for his lack of enthusiasm by exclaiming, 'My! You *do* look nice.'

'Not nice enough for some, it would appear,' Andrina said in a low voice as he went out to start the car.

Marion nodded and whispered. 'She wore a lot of that colour—that wife of his.'

Andrina groaned. So Drew had been expecting the moth and instead the butterfly had appeared. She almost ran back upstairs to change and then thought better of it. If Drew was going to let what she was dressed in blind him to the fact that she was nothing like his ex-wife, it was too bad...and when all was said and done, what was this evening about?

It was merely a gesture on his part. A fitting end to a very special day. Two people with similar outlooks having a quiet meal together. It certainly wasn't intended as a proper date. And fixing a smile on her face, she went out to join him.

'I take it that you think I'm overdressed,' she said coolly, as they drove along the hill road towards the country club where he'd booked the meal.

'I don't recall making such a comment,' he remarked levelly.

'No, but it's what you're thinking.'

'Does it matter what I'm thinking?'

That was a tricky one. If she said yes, he might think she was presuming too much. And if she said no, it could wipe out the rapport that had sprung up between them over recent weeks.

So she compromised with, 'It might.'

He sighed.

'When I saw you at the top of the stairs it was a shock, that's all. I'm used to seeing you looking…'

As he paused, searching for words, she had some of her own ready to fill the gap.

'Pale and insignificant?'

Laughter rumbled deep in his throat.

'Pale maybe, but insignificant...no way! I'll never forget how your hackles rose when I called at your apartment that first time, and there have been occasions since when you've shown great strength of will and determination.'

'And now here I am,' she said, not quite sure what she meant by it.

'Yes, here you are...and here am I. *I've* no regrets if you haven't.'

Her heartbeat was quickening. She glanced across at him, hoping to find in his expression what she wanted to see, but his next words took away the promise of what he'd just said.

'Our domestic set-up is ideal for the moment. By taking each day as it comes, I think we're coping very well. Obviously Jonathan won't be a baby for ever, but he's going to need us for a long time yet.'

She was becoming more attracted to him by the minute, Andrina thought bleakly, but there didn't seem to be any response coming from his direction. Could she face years of platonic living with Drew?

Aggravated by his reasoning, she said snappily, 'And what do we do if one of us wants to marry at some time in the future? It might all seem very simple now, but what would we do then?'

He sighed again. It was meant to be a relaxed evening, the two of them alone, unwinding after the day's events. But instead Andrina was raking up all sorts of things that he didn't want to think about.

'I suggest that we face that sort of problem if it arises,' he said, trying to conceal his exasperation. 'Unless *you* already have someone in mind.'

'Of course I haven't!' she protested angrily. 'My life is taken up between the house and the surgery. *You* are the one most likely to put us in that position.'

'Me!' His irritation was increasing. 'And what have I done to make you think that? Had the women of the village queuing up for my favours? One-night stands? Nights on the town? In case you haven't noticed, I spend most of my spare time covered in grime, renovating the farmhouse.'

This was ridiculous, Andrina thought. They were falling out over hypothetical problems, and it was all because she was wearing the dress. It had set the tone of the evening before it had even begun. She was letting the reception it got get to her, and the last thing she wanted was to quarrel with Drew over something so trivial. It was the harmony between them that had been the most wonderful part of their arrangement.

'I'm sorry,' she said softly. 'I don't know what's got into me. I'm being a pain. I was really looking forward to this evening but we seem to have got off on the wrong foot.'

The good humour that she so much admired in him came back, and he flashed her a smile as he said, 'Let's start again, shall we? Kiss and make up?'

Pulling up at the side of the road, he leaned across and brushed her cheek with his lips. She could smell tangy aftershave mixed with the smell of freshly showered male, and Andrina closed her eyes.

'What?' he asked. 'What's wrong?'

When she opened them he was so near their faces were almost touching, and as if her thoughts were mirrored in her wide hazel gaze, he kissed her again, on the mouth this time.

It was a gentle gesture as before. A mark of affection between friends. But after the first few seconds of contact it changed. He was reaching out for her, hands gripping her shoulders, and as they melted together it was as if their whole world was encompassed in the shadowed interior of the car.

'Whew!' he breathed when at last they drew apart. 'I had no intention of letting that happen.'

Andrina turned away. So he hadn't meant it. She'd just been taken on a fast trip to the stars and then dropped back to earth like a pricked balloon.

With what was left of her composure, she said lightly, 'Yes. It wasn't a good idea, was it? Our relationship is complicated enough. The last thing we need is to let our animal instincts take over.'

As he pulled back into the line of traffic Drew's face was sombre. That was one for him, he thought. It was *his* animal instincts Andrina had been referring to. She thought he'd just used her for a quick diversion.

It was true what he'd said, though. He'd had no intention of kissing her like that. Yet once he'd let his feelings take over it had been fantastic. She was the first woman he'd touched since Tania.

The perfume she was wearing was as fresh as flowers, compared to the heavy musk brands that his ex-wife used. With his mouth on hers she'd felt soft and pliant in his arms during those first few seconds, then it had changed and they'd been on fire.

Had it been because they were both starved of contact with the opposite sex? Whatever it was, Andrina had just put it into perspective and he had better cool it.

It was the dratted dress, she was thinking in the seat beside him. It reminded him of her. Because she'd turned out looking like a Tania look-alike it had switched him on. So he must still have some feelings for his ex-wife.

The restaurant was looming up in front of them and minutes later they were being shown to a table looking out over the starlit moors. Andrina thought wryly that they had the time, the setting and maybe, from what had happened earlier, the inclination, yet the night was spoilt and she felt like weeping.

But Drew's dark blue gaze was on her and pride wouldn't let her crumble in front of him. It had been an emotional day all round. The christening with no parents present. Being asked for a date for the first time in many months. And then tonight the dress...the argument...the kiss. She wished she could just go home and curl up under the covers. But a waiter was offering her a menu, and forcing a smile, she chose a safe subject to discuss—the surgery.

'I've been talking to James,' she said. 'Did you know that once he's passed his finals he intends working abroad with one of the relief agencies? I asked him if he had a girlfriend and he said, ''No, not a steady one. It wouldn't be fair to her if I was working abroad. We wouldn't see anything of each other.'' It seems those sentiments lasted until he did a home visit to someone called Suzanne Hamer, and now he's having second thoughts. Do you know her?'

'Yes. She's an attractive twenty year old suffering from myalgic encephalomyelitis— ME. It started a year ago after a viral infection that didn't clear up properly. Since then the poor girl has had all the symptoms. First of all there was severe muscle fatigue, followed by nausea, dizziness, pins and needles sensations and panic attacks, just to mention a few.'

She nodded.

'Yes, that's the girl. James said that before she'd been a bright, energetic medical student, and in spite of the fact that she'd called him out because she was having a really bad day, when she discovered that he'd taken the same course that she was struggling with she perked up. He offered to lend her some books to help with her course work and has wasted no time in calling round with them.'

'So you think that young James has been bitten by the love bug?' Drew said as they went into the lounge for coffee after an excellent meal.

'It's possible,' she replied. 'But it wasn't on the agenda. He wanted to steer clear of anything like that because of his future plans.'

'It's going to be a case of "Watch this space" then?'

'Something like that. It can bite when one least expects it, can't it?'

'What can?'

'The love bug.'

'Yes,' he agreed, and wondered if the pain of its bite was anything to do with the ache inside him.

CHAPTER FIVE

DREW had taken Marion home.

'I won't be long,' he'd said, and Andrina had known that the moment he was gone she was going to dash upstairs and take off the wretched dress. He was *not* going to find an exotic flower waiting for him when he got back, and minutes later she was seated at the kitchen table with face scrubbed clean, wrapped in a warm robe and sipping a mug of hot chocolate.

After the unsettling evening the sensible thing would have been to go straight to bed, but with her thoughts in turmoil she needed to see if Drew had any further comments to make before she tried to get some sleep.

When he came back and saw her sitting there, he smiled.

'You looked great tonight,' he said, 'but now you look more like the woman I know and...' He'd been going to say 'love' and was staggered that the word had come so easily to mind. But after that moment of madness earlier Andrina had made it clear that she wanted no further complications in her life and he supposed he couldn't blame her. Yet time would tell, and at the moment that was a commodity they had in plenty. Just as long as no third parties turned up out of the blue to spoil things.

They went up the stairs together and when they reached the landing they both halted before going to their separate rooms. Drew knew from the ache inside him that he wanted to kiss her again and take it from there, but these days he wasn't the impulsive person he'd been when he'd rushed into marriage to Tania. He'd learned what pain that sort of decision could bring. He could wait, and in any case, as he'd just been reminding himself, Andrina wanted things to stay as they were between them.

So with the smile that always made her heart beat faster, he said, 'It's been quite a day, hasn't it, Andrina? Shall we have a peep at Jonathan before we turn in?'

She nodded. Once again Drew had hit just the right note, and as they tiptoed into Jonathan's room she had that feeling again, as if the missing parents were somewhere in the ether close by, and she wanted to tell Jodie that it was all right…that she would love and care for her child as long as there was breath in her body.

'Do you think *they* know what we're doing?' he asked in a low voice, tuning into her thoughts as he gently lifted a tiny hand and tucked it beneath the covers.

'Yes, I'm sure they do,' she replied softly. She reached out and touched Drew's cheek for a fleeting moment. 'You saved my sanity the day you offered to help me care for him.'

His eyes had darkened but his voice was easy enough as he told her obliquely, 'You did the same for me. And with regard to more mundane matters, if we don't get to bed soon we'll be late for Monday morning surgery. We saw quite a few patients last week with flu symptoms and I wouldn't be surprised if there's an epidemic on the way. That'll keep us on our toes.'

With her hand on the handle of her bedroom door, she said, 'Thanks for organising the christening and taking me out to dinner. As you said, it's been quite a day and I won't forget one moment of it.'

'Good,' he said with the same easiness, hoping that the time they'd spent in each other's arms would be high on her list of memories, but he still had his feelings well under control, especially after those precious moments beside the baby's cot. It had seemed as if the three of them had been wrapped in a warm, close cocoon and he hadn't wanted to spoil it. Of late, there hadn't been many of those sorts of moments in his life.

During the week that followed the two doctors had little time to think about what was happening in their private lives as it seemed that the flu bug had indeed arrived, with a waiting room full all the time with pale-faced patients coughing and sneezing.

'October is early for a flu epidemic,' Drew said on the Monday evening, after a day of handing out flu jabs to those vulnerable people who hadn't yet had them, and examining those who had succumbed. His glance had been on the baby cooing happily in his cot and there'd been anxiety in it.

'I know what you're thinking,' Andrina told him. 'That the surgery is not the ideal place for Jonathan to be at the moment, even if he is kept well away from the patients. But, Drew, I can't stay at home with him. In a crisis such as this, we're both needed at the practice.'

'So we find someone to look after him during surgery hours until the outbreak is under control,' he'd said.

'Yes, but who? We can't ask Marion. She's in the same situation as us. She's needed at the surgery. And I can't see Eamon giving Jonathan his bottle in the middle of organising MOTs and car repairs. In any case, I wouldn't want him to.'

'There's a new day nursery opened in the village,' he said thoughtfully. 'Serena Smith has bought the old church hall and had it renovated. I'm sure that she would take him until things quieten down at the surgery. I'll go and see her after we've eaten. She has a flat above the premises.'

He was smiling when he came back.

'It's sorted. I've arranged that we'll drop Jonathan off on our way to the practice in the mornings and you will pick him up as soon as afternoon surgery is over, leaving James and me to clear up at the end of the day. Serena is well named. She's middle-aged, is calm and capable and is fully qualified to run such an establishment. She showed me round and the place is immaculate.'

Andrina felt a mixture of relief and anxiety when he'd explained what he'd arranged and said, 'I don't like the idea of Jonathan being away from us but I suppose in this sort of emergency we have to do what is best for *him*.'

'He'll be fine,' Drew had said. 'I feel the same as you, but it *is* the wisest arrangement under the circumstances.'

* * *

Later that evening, when he'd gone outside to do some work on one of the outhouses at the farm, Andrina sat gazing into the fire, deep in thought. There was no denying that in the early days she'd been extremely reluctant to accept the responsibility for Jodie's son, but ever since that never-to-be-forgotten night when she'd discovered that her stepsister had given birth to a little boy, Jonathan had never been far away, except for the previous evening when Drew had taken her to the country club.

Even during her working day at the practice he was close by, and although Drew did more than his share of caring for him when they were at home she was always near, watching over him, loving him so much that she ached with tenderness. And now they were having to hand him over to someone that she didn't know.

When they arrived at the church hall the next morning it was a scene of great activity. Parents were arriving with babies and toddlers, and two teenage girls in blue uniforms were receiving their small charges for the day.

'Where is Serena?' Drew asked one of them as he and Andrina hesitated on the fringe of the activity.

Her concerns were diminishing as she looked around her. The equipment was all new and spotless and the two assistants pleasant and capable-looking girls.

'I'm here,' a voice said from behind, and as Andrina swung round the woman that Drew had described was standing there, looking the picture of neat efficiency. In contrast, Andrina was feeling anything but organised after a restless night caused by thoughts of letting the baby out of her sight, and on top of that she'd had to dash upstairs to change after Jonathan had brought up all over her when she'd picked him up as they'd been on the point of leaving the farm.

'Your little one will be fine with us, Dr Bell,' she said. 'It's always a wrench, having to leave them the first time, but we'll take good care of him.'

Andrina nodded. It was the sensible thing they were doing. If it worked out all right, it might be a good idea to keep Jonathan away from the surgery on a regular basis.

As she handed him over to one of the young assistants, he gave the toothless smile that always made her heart twist.

'Please, take special care of him,' she said to the girl. 'This child is the light of my life.'

Bending over the baby, Andrina didn't see Drew's expression. If she had she might have thought that for a moment the doting uncle was missing and in his place was a sober-faced stranger.

Andrina was making no secret of her love for the child, and for a strange moment he was envious. It must be a wonderful feeling to be the light of someone's life, he thought as they went back out to the car, instead of featuring merely as bank balance and bedmate.

When they arrived at the practice there was no time for any more pondering. It was like it had been the previous day, and would continue to be so until the flu outbreak had run its course.

Yet Andrina's first patient hadn't got flu. Michael Rayner was in a very poor state of health due to acute liver failure. He was in and out of hospital frequently until such time as a transplant could be arranged.

The sixty-year-old's condition was due to having been given infected blood some years ago during an operation, and his health had slowly deteriorated ever since.

'My stomach is swollen again,' he said morosely, 'and I keep feeling drowsy and confused. I can see another spell in Intensive Care coming up if a liver isn't available soon.'

When Andrina examined him she saw that his stomach was indeed distended and they both knew why. Excess fluid forming in the abdomen was part of the condition, as was drowsiness and confusion, because of dysfunction of the brain. Unless a liver became available soon, he was going to die.

'I suspect that you have another infection,' she told him. 'It would account for the increase of fluid and the other symptoms. I know you don't want to hear it, but I do think we need to get you back in hospital, Mr Rayner. I could prescribe antibiotics but there is no guarantee that the infection would clear up with just that, and your condition can't be allowed to worsen. We need to have you under medical supervision all the time until there is some improvement.'

'Aye, all right,' he said wearily. 'I'll go home and get my things ready. My bag is still packed from the last time I was in, and then I'll phone for an ambulance.'

'Do you have someone who can accompany you to the hospital?'

He shook his head. 'My wife died last year and now the only kin I've got is my daughter, who lives down south. So, no, but I'm quite capable of managing on my own. I know the routine off by heart, I've been admitted so many times.'

'All right, then, but do, please, let the surgery know as soon as you're discharged. And, Mr Rayner?'

'What, Doctor?'

'Next time one of us will come to you. Just ring and ask for a visit.'

He gave a grim chuckle. 'I'm that bad, am I?'

Andrina had a smile for him. 'Let's just say that you're a very brave man.'

As she filled in his notes to record the visit, she was thinking that it would be bad enough for Michael if his condition was self-inflicted due to heavy drinking, but to have a diseased liver because of negligence in the system must be a very bitter pill to swallow. She prayed that soon an organ would become available. He deserved that chance.

When she arrived at the nursery in the late afternoon, leaving Drew to finish off all the odds and ends that the hectic day had brought, Jonathan smiled his little smile again when he saw her and her world righted itself. He was all right, she thought thankfully. Clean and well fed and obviously not fretting.

'Here he is,' Serena said as she handed him over. 'We'll look forward to seeing you both again tomorrow.'

Andrina nodded and told her, 'If any of the children appear unwell during the next couple of weeks, send for us. Alternatively, advise the parents to do so. It looks like we have a flu epidemic on our hands.'

'Don't worry. We will,' she said. 'Dr Curtis mentioned it last night. He's a charming man, isn't he?'

'Yes, he is,' Andrina agreed. Even old Mrs Carslake at the top cottage, wrinkled and bent with arthritis, had remarked the other day, 'It always gives me a lift, seeing Dr Curtis. If I was fifty years younger he would have to watch out.'

When Drew came striding in Jonathan was propped up on the sofa surrounded by cushions so that he wouldn't fall off. As always Drew went straight across to where he was.

'How did it go?' he asked as Jonathan cooed up at him.

'Fine,' she told him thankfully.

When they'd eaten, Drew said, 'I can't assist with Jonathan's bathtime tonight. I've brought some paperwork home with me that has to be done, and then I have to go out.'

Andrina was in the process of undressing the baby and when his tiny body was revealed Drew came to stand beside them.

'Beautiful,' he breathed, his glance taking in the woman who had learned to love someone else's child and the recipient of that love lying serenely in her arms.

But wrapped inside the stiff confines of a plastic apron, and wondering where Drew was off to after he'd done the paperwork, it never occurred to Andrina that the comment had been directed at her just as much as the baby, and breaking into the moment she enquired, 'Will you be out long?'

'Er…I might be. It all depends,' he said, still not offering to explain where he was going. 'It's something that I've been intending doing for a while and don't want to put it off any longer.' And that was it.

'You don't mind, do you?' he asked.

'No, of course I don't,' she said quickly. 'You don't have to ask my permission when you want to go out in the evening.'

'True. I *don't* have to ask your permission, but I *do* have to make sure that you haven't got anything planned yourself.'

That will be the day, she thought wryly, unless she wanted to take Eamon up on his offer, and she wasn't that desperate yet.

'It's only fair,' he was saying gravely. 'Because we're just as much partners in what goes on here as we are in the practice. Agreed?'

She smiled. When it came to sweet reason Drew was a past master, but why was he being so mysterious?

'Yes. Agreed,' she told him, and began to climb the stairs without further comment.

Watching her, Drew was gripped by a sudden feeling of uncertainty. They'd been in harmony until the day of the christening. Happy in what they were doing. Happy in what they were sharing. And he didn't want it to change. But it had and, memorable though it had been, he wished he hadn't kissed her.

Yet she'd kissed him back with equal passion, so he need have no guilt on that score. But it didn't alter the fact that they'd broken the unspoken terms of the agreement and, much as he had no wish to turn out on a chilly night to cross swords with his ex-wife, maybe a few hours away from Andrina wasn't a bad idea.

Jonathan would be talking eventually, Drew thought as he seated himself at the desk in the study and pulled the paperwork he'd brought home towards him. What would they do then? Teach him to call them Mummy and Daddy and when he was older explain the circumstances?

But supposing one of them had branched away before that time. How would they resolve that situation? They both loved Jonathan equally. He, Drew, was the blood relative, but it was Andrina who had taken him into her life when there had been no one else to do it.

There *was* a way to prevent that sort of situation occurring, but Andrina would probably think him a cold fish if he suggested it. *His* pulses were leaping at the very thought, but he didn't think Andrina would feel flattered if he proposed to her under the present circumstances.

Another problem was that once he'd said what was in his mind, what they had now would be gone for ever. He could shatter the idyll and find there was nothing to replace it with if she refused.

She'd reappeared in the doorway with Jonathan wrapped in a big white towel and when she saw his expression she asked, 'What's wrong? You look as if your lights have suddenly been put out.'

'I just had a thought that caused a minor power cut,' he said unsmilingly, and reaching out for the baby he pushed the paperwork to one side. As he looked down at his nephew he was asking himself if it *was* worth the risk. He could feel moisture on his brow. Supposing she said no? Supposing she said yes?

He supposed he had a nerve for even contemplating such a thing, and before he did anything else he had to sort Tania out. The present situation with his ex-wife just couldn't be allowed to continue.

*   *   *

What was all that about? Andrina wondered as she went into the kitchen to prepare Jonathan's bottle. She'd never seen Drew look so solemn. There'd been no signs of Tania in recent days so she didn't think it was anything to do with her, but she still felt that those two had some unfinished business.

She wished that just once in a while Drew could see herself as she really was. He only ever saw her surrounded by baby things, or behind her desk at the practice. On the one occasion when she could have made an impression she'd worn 'the dress' and reminded him of someone that he *said* he wanted to forget.

She fed Jonathan while Drew continued with the paperwork he'd brought home, and then took the baby up and settled him for the night. When she looked in on him a few minutes later he was fast asleep with one tiny fist tucked beneath his chin.

'He's well away,' Drew's voice said from behind her, and when she turned she saw that he'd changed and was ready to go out.

'I'll see you later,' he said casually. 'Don't wait up.'

'I won't. Have no fear,' she told him, knowing that she sounded snappy.

His sombre expression of earlier came back for a moment but he shrugged it off and with a wave of the hand went striding down the stairs as if he couldn't wait to get out into the night.

The moment he'd gone the curiosity she'd been holding in check leapt forth. Instead of curling up on the sofa as she would have done if he'd been there, Andrina wandered from room to room restlessly, until she realised that she was behaving like a doubting wife and flopping down in front of the fire she sat gazing into its embers.

The heat from it was making her drowsy and she was on the brink of dozing when she heard Jonathan's cry. It was a chesty sort of wail, not a bit like his usual lusty yell and it brought her back to full consciousness in a flash.

When she picked him up she could feel fever in him. His cheeks were flushed, his eyes bright, and in spite of being a doctor she was just as panic-stricken as any other loving mother on seeing their infant poorly.

Andrina wasn't aware of it but Tania had appeared at the surgery shortly after she'd left to collect Jonathan that afternoon. She'd been her usual strident, outrageous self and had only been willing to leave when Drew had agreed to call round that evening to discuss a proposition she wanted to put to him.

It was the last thing he wanted to do, spend time with her when he could be with Andrina and the baby, but it would give him the opportunity to make her realise once and for all that she was not in his life any more. The fact that she thought that she could be said a lot for her incredible arrogance, but tonight she was going to get the message, he thought grimly as he pulled up in front of her parents' house.

They were a pleasant elderly couple and well respected in the community, which was more than could be said for their daughter.

He was wishing now that he'd told Andrina where he was going, but he knew instinctively that if he had she would have got the wrong idea and he hadn't wanted that to happen.

Tania was dressed to go out when she opened the door to him and, pulling it to behind her, she said, 'Let's go to the Grouse. I don't want to talk in front of my parents.'

'All right,' he agreed reluctantly. 'Hop in.'

When they'd settled themselves in a quiet corner Drew said flatly, 'So what do you want to talk about, Tania?'

'Us of course,' she said wheedlingly in the husky voice that grated on him so much these days.

'There is nothing to discuss. I've told you a thousand times, we're finished.'

'You haven't heard what I have to say,' she protested. 'I want us to get back together, Drew, and as you seem so set on having a kid of your own I'm willing to oblige.'

That brought back the cold anger that had torn him apart before, and he told her, 'You don't listen, do you? How many times do I have to tell you that I want nothing more to do with you? I do want children of my own, but not with you, Tania, never with you. And in the meantime I'm totally happy looking after my nephew.'

'And having an unpaid nursemaid thrown in helps, no doubt,' she snarled. 'I can't see you fancying her for anything else. Not when you've had someone like me.'

Goaded by her conceit, he told her, 'Compared to Andrina you are nothing. I want you out of my life permanently and the sooner you realise that the better.'

He got to his feet.

'I'm going, Tania. I have better things to do.' And leaving her fuming and frustrated he went, but not to return to the farm. He needed time to cool down. His ex-wife was the only person he'd ever met who could enrage him to such a degree. She was willing to oblige, he thought furiously. *Willing* to give him a child. Big deal!

He turned on to the hill road and once he was up on the moors stopped in a lay-by and sat staring into the starlit night for what seemed an eternity. Then at last, feeling calmer in spirit, he drove home to the place where he was happiest.

When he got back to Whistler's Farm Drew was surprised to see that the lights were still on. When he went inside he found Andrina pacing up and down with the fretful baby in her arms.

'What's wrong?' he asked immediately.

Because of her anxiety and the fact that he'd been out when she'd needed him, she was less than pleasant in her reply.

'Jonathan's got a temperature,' she cried. 'How could we not have noticed that he wasn't well before he was put down for the night?'

'Steady on,' he said equably. 'We didn't notice because he was fine. Whatever is wrong with him has obviously come on since. If I'd thought he was sickening for something I wouldn't have gone out.'

The clock on the wall indicated that it was half past one and, still frazzled, Andrina said,

'I'm surprised that you bothered coming home. Why didn't you go straight to the surgery? This is the result of taking him to the nursery. We should have realised that he was more likely to pick something up there than anywhere.'

She knew that she was being unreasonable but she couldn't help it. It was due partly to Drew having been wherever he'd gone for so long, but the main reason was her concern over Jonathan, the fact that he'd become ill so quickly.

Ignoring her comments, Drew said levelly, 'What have you given him?'

'Just infant paracetamol. Because I'm not sure what it is. Do you think it could be the flu bug?'

'Have you sounded his chest? Remember, he's not had the whopping cough vaccine yet.'

'Yes. It wasn't clear but there was nothing to suggest that.'

'Good. Because there's a lot of it about, mainly because of fear of a bad reaction on the part of parents. Give him to me, Andrina. I'll see if I can get him to sleep and will have him in my room tonight.'

'I'm quite capable of looking after him,' she told him with the snappiness still present.

He sighed. 'Did I say you weren't? If all this is because I've been out for a few hours, maybe I'd better remind you that we are both free agents. You don't own me, and I don't own you. So let's not let the situation get out of hand.'

'I'm sorry,' she mumbled. 'The doctor in me has been overtaken by the anxious parent.'

What on earth was he saying? Drew wondered. It would have been an ideal moment to put the question that had been foremost in his mind all the time he'd been listening to Tania's arrogance, and instead he'd pushed them further apart.

As soon as he felt himself up against the firm warmth of Drew's chest, Jonathan closed his eyes and went to sleep. Although she was relieved to see it, it didn't make Andrina feel any less fractious.

Jonathan often slept through the night now, but as Drew carried him carefully upstairs she said, 'I'll make up a bottle just in case.'

'Yes, do that,' he agreed unsmilingly, 'and then go to bed yourself. I'm in charge.'

It was as if he was saying, Make yourself scarce. I've heard enough from you for tonight.

So she did just that, but not to sleep. She may have been sent packing but it didn't mean that she was taking a back seat. Not if her precious child might need her.

Twice she tiptoed into Drew's room to check on the baby and found the man himself watching her from where he lay against the pillows, fully awake.

'He's all right, Andrina,' he said the second time. 'The paracetamol has brought his temperature down and he's breathing easier. It could be early teething. Go back to bed. You *can* trust me, though anyone hearing you earlier wouldn't have thought so.

'If you want to know where I've been, I had something to discuss with Tania. We needed to talk. Obviously if I'd known Jonathan

wasn't well I would have come back immediately. Does that satisfy you?'

'You don't have to explain,' she told him
flatly, as all the implications of what he was
saying came crowding in on her. 'As I've already said, I'm sorry for kicking up such a
fuss.'

'Don't be,' he said gently. 'I wish I'd been
here.'

Andrina didn't reply. With a last look at
Jonathan she went back to her room and once
more beneath the covers lay wide-eyed and
forlorn.

She'd been right, she told herself as the
minutes ticked by. The flame *did* still burn between those two. Tania may be a madam, but
she herself couldn't compete with her when it
came to sex appeal. Had Drew forgiven her
and during the hours he'd been absent they'd
been discussing what to do about the situation
here at the farm if they got back together
again?

If that *was* the case, he had a short memory
and would deserve all he got, she thought mis-

erably as she tossed and turned. But Drew was worthy of better than that. She loved him, and couldn't bear to think of him being hurt again.

She'd finally admitted it and it came as no surprise. How could she help loving him? Just to be near him was joy. Why couldn't everything stay as it was?

CHAPTER SIX

ANDRINA was up first the next morning. When she looked into Drew's room he was asleep still on top of the covers and Jonathan was gazing around him in his cot looking almost back to normal. Whatever had been the cause of the previous night's discomfort he seemed to have got over it.

As her heart leapt with thankfulness, all the worry and frustrations she'd experienced then came flooding back. The baby's sudden fever during Drew's absence. His meeting with Tania that had lasted so long. Only lovers would want to be with each other for that length of time, she thought bleakly.

As she carried the baby downstairs she saw that he was still pale in spite of being so much better, and she eyed him anxiously.

Passing the door of the study where Drew had been working the previous evening, she saw that some of the papers he'd been dealing with had drifted off the desk and she bent to pick them up.

The one uppermost was a solicitor's letter if the heading was anything to go by, and as she put it back on the desktop the first line of the communication caught her eye and, unable to stop herself, she read on.

It seemed that Drew had been in touch with them about adopting his nephew and was seeking advice on all the legal pros and cons.

Andrina sank down slowly onto the nearest chair.

It was all fitting together like a jigsaw puzzle, she thought fearfully. Last night's rendezvous with Tania, the solicitor's letter. He was going to have his ex-wife back and was considering making his relationship with Jonathan rock solid. And where would that leave her? Out in the cold?

When Drew came down to breakfast he smiled when he saw the baby tucking into his cereal.

'Another crisis over, then,' he said with a quick glance at Andrina's set face.

'Yes. Jonathan's chest is clear, but he's still pale,' she told him tightly.

'He *is* going to look pale after his flushed cheeks of last night,' he said mildly.

Still edgy, she replied, 'Yes, I know that. But it doesn't alter the fact that I don't like the idea of leaving him.'

The words had come out mechanically. She was still feeling dazed from reading the letter not meant for her eyes.

He sighed. 'Look, Andrina, you can't wrap him up in cotton wool. Children gain a degree of immunity by contact with other people. We all do. So let's calm down, shall we?'

Calm down? she felt like shrieking back at him. She'd never felt less calm in her life. It was as if the ground had been taken from under her feet. If Drew thought he was going to take Jonathan from her and let that woman be involved in his upbringing, he had another think coming. The thought that he could contemplate such a thing was tearing her apart.

But she had no claim on him, except for loving him more than life itself. She wouldn't have a leg to stand on if it came to a court ruling.

'Don't patronise me, Drew,' she said, bringing her thoughts back to what was being said. 'I suppose you think that I've gone from one extreme to the other, from not wanting Jodie's child in the first instance to smothering him with affection. If that *is* the case, I think I could be excused as I've never neglected him in any way since the moment I took charge of him.'

'Don't you think I'm aware of that?' he parried. 'What is it with you? Have I done something to upset you?'

Andrina swallowed hard. She was tempted to break the rules they had set themselves and tell him that she was in love with him. That *she* would love and cherish him if he would let her. Instead, she said the first thing that came into her head, and as soon as the words were out she knew it had been a mistake.

'When you came in last night you said that you'd been with Tania.'

He was observing her with raised brows.

'So that's what is bugging you. Yes, I had. So what's the problem? As I hadn't a crystal ball with me at the time, I didn't know anything was wrong and, having left Jonathan in good health, I didn't feel the need to report in.'

Still driven to put the blight on the morning she said, 'You must have had a lot to discuss.'

He'd been fixing his tie in front of the hall mirror but now he was swivelling round to face her.

'Nothing of the kind. It was all done and dusted within minutes.'

So what had he and Tania been doing for the rest of the time? she wondered. *Were* they back on a friendly footing with so much to catch up on that the hours had flown?

Drew's expression was giving nothing away and she wasn't going to ask.

'Let's get the show under way, shall we?' he said, as if what had gone before was of no consequence. 'As you are still concerned about

Jonathan, I suggest that you call in at the nursery between surgeries just to satisfy yourself that he's all right.'

'I have every intention of doing so,' she told him, feeling more left out than ever.

Why did she have to fall in love with him? she thought as they drove to the church hall, and knew she didn't have to look for an answer. He was everything she'd ever dreamed of, but was life ever that simple?

During those first weeks at the farm she'd been totally happy. The relief of having someone to turn to had been exquisite, as had been knowing that Jonathan was out of the high-rise apartment and living in the beautiful countryside.

Drew had ironed out all her problems and there hadn't been a cloud in her sky during the past weeks, but now he was complicating everything. She should have known from the start that a man as attractive as Drew was going to affect her senses sooner or later, and because of him being what he was it had been sooner rather than later. But it looked as if the chance of him returning her feelings was nil.

He'd put her longings into perspective last night when he'd told her that they were both free agents. In other words *his* feelings towards *her* were no different than they'd been at the start.

When they arrived at the nursery she told Serena, 'Jonathan wasn't well last night. Please, keep a special eye on him, will you?'

The other woman had heard the story of how the baby had come to be where he was and she said with a smile, 'That sister of yours chose well when she left her child in your care, Dr Bell. Of course we'll keep an eye on him. What was it? Temperature? Chesty? There's a lot of it about.'

Drew nodded. 'Yes, there is. Winter isn't even here and we're in the thick of it already. The holly is laden with berries and so early, too. We country folk say it's a sign of a hard winter.'

Andrina was thinking about the solicitor's letter and was only half listening. Her mind was still grappling with what she'd read earlier. Shock and anger were making her feel disorientated, and as they drove to the surgery she said absently, 'What was it you were saying about the holly?'

'I said that it's laden with berries. More so than I've ever seen it. Old Eli Thompson, who lives by the reservoirs, was only saying the other day when he came to the surgery that there's going to be weather to treat with respect once the winter has settled in, and he's not usually wrong in his forecasts.

'I remember we had some hard winters when we were kids. But I didn't notice them so much at the time. If it snowed we were in heaven. But I can remember when a couple were trapped up on the tops in a blizzard and nearly froze to death. It will be no joke being out and about, visiting our patients, if we get that sort of weather again.'

'Mmm,' she said, still feeling traumatised.

'You're miles away,' he protested. 'I hope you're not still dwelling on last night.'

Andrina pulled herself together. A busy day lay ahead of them and lack of concentration was not permissible in their profession.

'No, of course not,' she told him flatly, and wished she sounded more convincing.

'Good. Because we have more important things to think about than a minor squabble.'

Drew was right, she thought grimly. Compared to what was coming, last night *would* seem like a minor upset. And if he was expecting her to ask what he meant, he was to be disappointed. At that moment she felt least said soonest mended and changed the subject. Time to have the big showdown when she'd gathered her wits.

'What was wrong with old Eli?' she asked with a quick change of subject. 'I've heard people speak of him but haven't yet met the village's oldest inhabitant.'

Drew laughed. 'He had nothing wrong with him. That's just the point. Other than a bout of wishful thinking.'

'I'm not with you.'

'Eli is considering getting married again and wanted to know if I thought it advisable as he's ninety-four next birthday.'

'Really! Some people never give up, do they? There are those of us who haven't even got started on the matrimonial merry-go-round and he's ready to try it again. I'm told that he's been to the altar three times already.'

'Yes. Maybe it's because of this cold winter that he says is coming and he wants someone to snuggle up to.'

'Who's the lucky woman?'

'A lady he met at Blackpool during the summer.'

'Did he ask for Viagra?'

'Not in so many words, but he did want to know if I thought he'd be up to it.'

'And what did you say?'

'He's a tough, wily, old peasant. What could I say?'

'Right. So there's going to be a wedding in the village.'

'No. It's all fallen through.'

'Why is that?'

'The bride-to-be objected to his ferrets. Eli has always kept ferrets and he gave her an ultimatum. It was either love me love my ferrets, or the wedding's off.'

They were still smiling at the antics of the elderly when they arrived at the practice and found the other world that they shared waiting for them.

Before either of them had the chance to ring for their first patients, a call came through on Drew's phone from the daughter of Michael Rayner, the patient with liver failure.

'That's excellent,' Andrina heard him say. 'We hope that all goes well. Give your father our best wishes.

'They've found a liver for Michael Rayner,' he said as he replaced the receiver. 'Let's hope it's not too late. That was his daughter. They did keep him in when you sent him to hospital and at the moment he's very poorly. But if they can keep him alive long enough to receive the transplant, there could be hope for him. Just as long as his body doesn't reject the new organ.'

'That's excellent news,' she said, and thought thankfully that at least something good was happening to someone.

'When are they operating?'

'Today. Now.'

'Brilliant.'

Not so brilliant was the state of the foot of a young housewife. It was swollen and inflamed, with the discoloration spreading up her leg.

'I stepped on a rusty nail in the garden shed,' she explained, 'and although I bathed the punctured area with hot water and antiseptic it started to get sore. Probably because I've never been good at fighting infection. My jaw's a bit stiff and it isn't easy to swallow at the moment. That couldn't have anything to do with the infection, could it?'

Alarm bells were ringing.

'Have you ever had an anti-tetanus injection?' Andrina asked.

'Yes, but not recently. It was about twelve years ago.'

'So you haven't received a letter from us asking you to come in for a booster, with it being so long since you had the initial injection?'

The woman shook her head.

'No. But I've recently moved house and I don't think the surgery has my new address.'

'Right. Well, that omission is about to be rectified immediately,' she told the patient. 'You have some of the symptoms of tetanus, which, as you are probably aware, is a condition not to be neglected under any circumstances.'

'I'm not going to lose my foot, am I?' she exclaimed fearfully.

'Not if we act immediately, but there *is* blood poisoning present and it is moving up your leg. Tetanus antitoxin injections are going to be needed to clear the infection and under the circumstances I would prefer you to be treated in hospital in case the infection worsens before it gets a chance to react to the treatment.'

'Whew! I should have come to see you sooner, shouldn't I?'

'Yes. But infections such as this can change from not so serious to very serious in a short time.'

When Andrina mentioned the tetanus patient to Drew at the end of morning surgery he frowned.

'When will the general public get wise to the danger of that sort of infection?' he said. 'I can remember when I was a kid my dad being called out to a farmer's wife with a badly swollen hand. Her wedding ring had got too tight and her husband had sawn it off with a rusty little handsaw. Tetanus was well and truly present, and though Dad had her admitted to hospital immediately she died. And now, on a lighter note, are you going to check on Jonathan, as I suggested?'

'Who's fussing now?' she asked.

'The other half of the partnership,' he called over his shoulder as he went out into the chilly morning to start his house calls.

Feeling somewhat comforted because he'd let her see that he didn't really think she'd been overreacting, she went to do as he'd suggested.

When she got there Jonathan was fine. One of Serena's young assistants was giving him his bottle and when he saw her he let the teat go slack for a moment and smiled.

Her world righted itself. She bent and kissed the baby's satin-smooth cheek and departed. On her way back to the surgery she phoned Drew to let him know that all was well.

'Great,' he said, and she could tell by his voice that he was smiling. 'So have I got my sane and sensible partner back?'

'Don't bank on it,' she told him coolly, and before he had time to react she rang off.

Drew was considering the future. Like Andrina, he was feeling that their relationship had changed in the last few days and was telling himself that he'd been crazy to think that it wouldn't, with the two of them living in such close proximity.

Compared to his ex-wife, Andrina was like a slender, brown-haired, focal point in both his life and Jonathan's. They needed her... desperately. He had his own strengths and would always be there for her and the baby, but he wasn't invincible as he was still bruised and smarting from his disastrous marriage to Tania. Yet he didn't blame her entirely. He couldn't believe that he'd let just mere sexual attraction propel him into matrimony.

And now what was he contemplating? Another catastrophe that had an even more crazy purpose to it than when he'd rushed into wedlock with Tania? More than anything he wanted Jonathan's future to be secure, but for that to happen the little one needed both of those who loved him to be permanently in his life.

He was thinking seriously of adoption, but hadn't yet discussed it with Andrina because he knew how fiercely possessive she was of Jonathan. He'd had to tread carefully a few times himself with regard to that and didn't want to do anything to upset her.

Yet he couldn't believe she would disagree with what he had in mind. They were a team now and, with his ring on her finger and Jonathan legally theirs, life could only get better.

Soon he was going to tell her what he had in mind, and that would be crunch time. He could feel it in his bones.

In the dark hours of recent nights he'd known how he wanted the road ahead to be. There *was* only one way to achieve complete stability for his nephew. The certainty of it became stronger with each passing day, as did the feeling that Jonathan wouldn't be the only one to be truly blessed if Andrina agreed to what he had in mind.

As he drove out of the village to visit a patient at a farm in one of the more remote parts of the area, Drew kept seeing Tania in the distance on horseback and knew with weary certainty that what he'd said the night before had fallen on deaf ears.

When he turned off onto a rough track that led to the home of his patient she came up from behind and reined in beside the car, forcing him to stop. He wound the window down and eyed her grimly. Whatever she wanted of him, she was wasting her time. But she was so unpredictable, so sure of her appeal it was like talking to a brick wall.

She was bending to face him from her high perch. Speaking in the wheedling tone that set his teeth on edge, she said, 'If you don't want a child from me any more, fair enough. We can pretend that the one you're looking after is ours and start from there.'

There were no words to answer that prime piece of cheek so he just shook his head and wound the window up again, set the car in motion once more and left her there.

As he parked beside a stone farmhouse of a similar size to his own, Drew was imagining what Andrina would have said if she'd heard that last preposterous suggestion from his ex-wife.

Woe betide anyone casting covetous eyes on Jonathan. He, Drew, had had to prove his own worth before she'd trusted him completely. As for Tania, she was the last person Jonathan's guardian angel would allow near the child.

Mavis Catchpole, the seventy-year-old farmer's wife, had suffered a minor stroke. It was evident the moment Drew saw her. Her speech was jumbled and confused, her eyes unfocused and she was dribbling from the side of her mouth.

'I came in from milking,' her husband said agitatedly while Drew was examining her, 'and found her like this.'

'Your wife has had a transient ischaemic attack,' Drew told him, 'or in simple terms, a mini-stroke. Her blood pressure is up. We need to get it down immediately. Have you any aspirin in the house?'

The man nodded.

'Give her two straight away and I will drop off a prescription at the chemist for further medication. I'll ask them to deliver it so that you don't need to leave her, and in the mean-time another two aspirin in a couple of hours.'

'But she can't talk.'

'Her speech may come back. At the moment it is hard to tell just how badly affected she is, but it *is* a minor stroke. She appears to have full use of all her limbs so there is no paralysis present. I'll be back to see her in a couple of days. In the meantime, keep a close watch on her and if there is any sign of a repeat of to-day's happenings send for an ambulance.'

On his way back to the practice a call came through on his mobile from the Brewster house and he groaned. It was Tania *again*. She must have gone straight home and was on the phone to him the minute she'd got in. But as he lis-tened to what she had to say, his expression altered.

'I've just got in,' she was explaining, 'and found Daddy on the floor. He's barely breathing. I don't know what to do. How soon can you get here?'

'Have you sent for an ambulance?' he asked tersely.

'No. Not yet.'

'I'll be with you in five minutes,' he promised, and increased his speed.

Tim Brewster had suffered a cardiac arrest and had stopped breathing altogether by the time he got there. The tell-tale blueness around the mouth, clammy skin and extreme pallor were signs enough.

'How long is it since he stopped breathing?' Drew asked Tania urgently as he flung himself down beside her father.

'Just before you got here,' she wailed.

'Right. Get an ambulance, tell them it's urgent. I'm going to do cardiopulmonary resuscitation.

'Your father has had a cardiac arrest,' he told her as he kept on with the CPR. 'When the ambulance arrives the paramedics will apply defibrillation, then they'll take him into Coronary Care. Where's your mother?'

'Out shopping, I think,' she said weakly.

'Better keep an eye open for her, then. Or she might be next if she sees the ambulance on the drive.'

He was fond of Tania's elderly parents. He'd never had any quarrel with *them*. If they'd been younger they might have been able to handle her, but she rode roughshod over them every time there was an argument and always got her own way in the end.

But not with him any more. Never again with him.

Angela Brewster still wasn't back when the ambulance came for her husband, and when Tania begged Drew to go to hospital with her he didn't refuse. He couldn't just leave the pair of them to it. He knew from past experience that Tania was not at her best in hospital surroundings.

On the way there he phoned Andrina at the practice to tell her that he wouldn't be back in time for afternoon surgery.

'Why, what's wrong?' she asked in the same clipped tone that she'd used earlier.

'Tania's father has had a major heart attack,' he told her. 'I'm going to the hospital with her for moral support. James should be able to manage on his own for once. I know *you'll* be anxious to pick Jonathan up as soon as possible after last night's problem.'

'Shouldn't her mother be with her?' she asked, 'rather than an outsider?'

He gave a dry laugh. 'I'm hardly an outsider. Tim and Angela still think of me as their son-in-law…and they're not the youngest of people by any means.'

'I'll see you when I see you, then,' she said dismissively, and replaced the receiver.

It went with what was already happening in the background, she thought miserably. Drew being there for Tania and her parents. He must have thought *her* attitude rather churlish, but after the hours he'd spent with his ex-wife the night before and this morning's discovery of the letter she didn't want any more reminders of his link with that family.

What *was* she going to do about it all? she kept asking herself. If it came to a confrontation with Drew over Jonathan, was she going to stay around and watch him be taken away from her? No way!

What, then? Move out of the farm and buy somewhere local for herself and the baby. Or go back to Gloucester. Ask for her old job back and do the best she could for the two of them. If the worst came to the worst, she would have to go into hiding, as no way was that woman going to be part of Jonathan's life.

Drew was another matter. He really loved him. She had no doubts on that score, but he wouldn't be around twenty-four hours a day and that was when Jonathan would be at risk.

She loved them both, the man and the child, and couldn't understand how Drew could be so underhanded as to plot to take him from her. He'd coaxed her into coming to this place and was now apparently contemplating managing without her. If that *was* the case, he was in for a big surprise she thought grimly.

As she was leaving the practice to pick up Jonathan, Marion said, 'We've just heard that Tim Brewster has had a heart attack. Is that where Dr Curtis is?'

Andrina nodded. 'Yes. He is at the hospital with them. I've spoken to James and he's taking the late surgery. There aren't too many appointments and I've told him to ring me if he has any problems. It's fortunate that the flu outbreak is slackening off or it would be a different matter.'

It was six o'clock in the evening when Andrina heard Drew's car pull up on the drive, and when she opened the door to him it was like meeting a sombre stranger for the first time. There was no warmth in his glance and the feeling that now he was here nothing could be as bad as it seemed dwindled away as she asked, 'Have you eaten?'

He shook his head. 'I'm not hungry.'

'But it must be hours since you had anything.'

'I said I'm not hungry,' he told her tonelessly. 'I've just been to the Brewsters' place to pick up my car, then I'm going back to the hospital as I'm worried about Angela. I thought that she was going to be the next one to collapse when she heard about what had happened to Tim. I've only stopped by to let you know what's going on.'

'I see.' So he'd merely called to put the real 'outsider' in the picture. She supposed she should be grateful that it hadn't been just a phone call. 'They are fortunate to have you there for them at such a time,' she said stiltedly.

'Maybe,' he replied absently, and then added in a more decisive tone, 'I only know that I have to give them my support.' He was already turning to go. 'Don't wait up. I have my key.'

When he'd gone and she'd shut out the cold night once more, Andrina went back to her thoughts. She'd never felt more lonely than she did at that moment.

She went into the study and picked up the solicitor's letter, which was still where she'd placed it, and read it again. As she did so she justified the action by deciding that as she'd already been guilty of a breach of good manners once, a second time couldn't make much difference.

It read the same. Drew had told his solicitor that he was thinking of adopting his nephew and that another party could be involved, and after outlining various legal aspects of the procedure he'd been advised who to get in touch with.

As she put the letter back where it had been, it was clear from the wording that so far Drew was just making initial enquiries. That no move towards that end had yet been made. But the mere fact that he was considering it was enough. She wasn't going to stand by and do nothing and then find it was too late to stake *her* full claim.

It was laughable that she'd let herself fall in love with Drew, hoping that he might feel the same about her, when all the time he'd had a different end in view. She was becoming more aware that he had other agendas as well as the arrangement they had here at the farm.

As Drew drove back to the hospital his thoughts were as dismal as Andrina's, but from a different viewpoint. He was happy to do all he could for Tania's parents. It was true what he'd said to Andrina. They did still look upon him as their son-in-law, and until the hazel-eyed doctor and Jodie's child had appeared on the scene he'd had no cause to upset them any more than they'd already been by the divorce.

But it was all going to have to change once he'd seen them through this. He and Andrina deserved a life of their own and the Brewsters, Tania first and foremost, were going to have to get on with their lives without him.

Today's emergency had come out of the blue and he wasn't going to stand back and let them cope alone, but once Tim was back on his feet and he'd made sure that Angela was coping, that would be it.

When Andrina had opened the door to him and the warmth of his home had reached out to him, he hadn't gone inside because he'd known that if he did he wouldn't want to go out again. He wanted to be with her and Jonathan. He always would. Nothing would change that. But she was uptight about something and if she wasn't asleep when he got back he would persuade her to tell him what was wrong.

It was half past eleven when he arrived back at the farm. They'd left Tim in the coronary unit, where he was being carefully monitored, and he'd driven Angela home to where Tania, who'd left them earlier, was prowling around the place like a caged lion.

'I can't stand those places,' she'd said fretfully when they'd got back, and he'd thought that typically she was putting herself first again.

He'd then made sure that her mother took a sedative as she was still in shock from discovering that her husband had suffered a heart attack while she'd been out shopping.

On leaving, he'd told Tania, 'Look after your mother. For once think of someone else besides yourself. I'll come back tomorrow to see how she is and will keep in touch with the hospital regarding your father. Now I'm going home.'

Although he'd told Andrina not to wait up, he was relieved to see that the light was still on in her bedroom and as he climbed the stairs she came out onto the landing in her night-dress.

'Hello,' he said wearily. 'I thought you'd be asleep.'

'Are you joking?' she exclaimed. 'How could I go to sleep when you were still with the Brewsters?'

'There was no need for you to be con-cerned,' he said tonelessly. 'Tania's parents are the ones to be worried about. She takes scant notice of them, but if they weren't there she would be in a mess.'

'She would still have you,' she said coolly.

He didn't deny it, merely said flatly, 'That is not the point.'

'I would have thought that it was.'

He was observing her wearily. 'You're still annoyed about something, aren't you? But let's wait until the morning, shall we? I'm too bogged down with one thing and another to discuss anything coherently at the moment. I'm going to have a peep at Jonathan and then I'm going to bed.'

She nodded and without further comment went back into her room and closed the door.

What a ghastly day it had been, Drew thought as he climbed out of his clothes. He just could not get free of the Brewsters. He'd no sooner made it clear to Tania that he wanted her out of his life permanently than her father's heart attack was bringing them into close contact again.

He thanked God for the woman in the room across the landing. He knew where he stood with Andrina. There were no complexities in her nature. She was a wonderful mother to Jonathan, a caring friend to himself and one day he hoped to cement their relationship into something deep and abiding. At the moment something was upsetting her, but once that was ironed out and he could free himself from his duty to the Brewsters, they might be able to get on with their own lives.

Tired as he was, it hadn't escaped his noticed out there on the landing that she looked just as beautiful in a sensible cotton nightgown, with her hair tousled and the dark smudges of sleeplessness beneath her eyes, as she had on the night she'd worn the flame silk dress. He'd given her the impression he didn't like her in it when all the time his lack of approval had stemmed from the fear that he might be walking the same path with her that he'd walked with Tania. Though he'd soon been reminding himself that Andrina would never be like Tania if she lived to be a hundred.

CHAPTER SEVEN

THE next morning Drew went into the study as soon as he came downstairs, and as Andrina watched she saw him pick up the letter from on top of the pile and push it beneath paperwork in one of the drawers of the desk.

'You're too late,' she said stonily. 'I've read it.'

He turned to face her with raised brows.

'You've read my private correspondence,' he said in cold amazement.

'The letter was on the floor so I picked it up. The first line caught my eye and, yes, I read on, and as I did a lot of things slotted into place.'

'Such as?' he demanded in the same tone.

'Your sudden desire for Tania's company. But let me tell you I will fight you all the way on Jonathan, Drew. I would trust *you* with him any time, but not her. Not that woman. As far

as I'm concerned, she's bad news. I can't believe that you could be such a fool as to risk
being hurt again.'

If his manner had been chilly before, now it
was like ice forming between them.

'Not bad,' he said tightly. 'In the space of a
few seconds you've made it clear that you see
me as deceitful, a breaker of promises and a
fool. No doubt there are other criticisms you
have of me, but before you launch into them,
may I remind you that I once told you I never
say anything that I don't mean and that in-
cludes me telling you that I would never come
between Jonathan and you? But it would appear you've forgotten that. Or else you've got
me down as a liar as well.

'I take it that when you read my correspondence you understood that I had merely begun
to make enquiries about adoption, nothing
else.'

'Maybe. What I *did* understand was that you
had started on that track without telling me.
That I was the odd one out and Tania, you and
Jonathan are to be a cosy little trio.'

'If that is the case, your opinion of me is even lower than I thought,' he said grimly. 'You'll have your answer to that in coming events, or the lack of them. I suggest that you take your accusations and bin them because you're wrong. In any future dealings we have with each other, I shall bear in mind that we have a no-trust situation, which suits me fine. Just as long as Jonathan doesn't suffer in the process.'

He went into the hall and reached for his briefcase and topcoat, and as she stood by, now lost for words, he told her, 'I'll skip breakfast. I have a nasty taste in my mouth.'

As he drove to the practice Drew was thinking grimly that he'd made a nice mess of things by leaving the letter on view. His idea had been to present Andrina with a package of promises that was made up of his love for her, his love for Jonathan and the framework, already in motion, for the two of them to adopt Jonathan.

Maybe he'd had a lucky escape. After all the weeks of closeness they'd shared she still thought he had hidden motives. It hurt…a lot. He knew now that he'd made a mistake wanting it to come as a surprise when he told her about the adoption. It would have been better if he'd included her from the start.

But what did it matter now? He'd lost the taste for it, had never felt so sickened in his life. Andrina must have been watching him all the time, he thought sombrely, and as far as she was concerned she'd caught him out.

When she arrived at the practice some time later, having dropped Jonathan off at the nursery, Drew was already seeing his patients, even though it was barely half past eight. She thought miserably that it had gone, the thing that she'd cherished so much—the companionship and trust that had made their unusual domestic set-up so successful.

Where did they go from here? she wondered. She hadn't needed Drew to put her out in the cold, she'd managed to do it very well herself. But the patients in the waiting room were eyeing her expectantly and, going into her room, she rang for the first one.

It was Michael Rayner's daughter, come to tell her that her father was already looking better, his yellow pallor beginning to diminish. It was early days, but no sign of rejection as yet.

When she'd thanked the woman for letting her know and bade her a cheerful goodbye, Andrina felt her spirits lifting. The dark divide that had sprung up between Drew and herself couldn't be allowed to blight everything. There was hope in Michael Rayner's life once more, and in their own lives there was still Drew's unconditional love of Jonathan. If *she* had fallen from grace, he hadn't.

He had been consumed with cold anger at her accusations but he hadn't offered any explanation. So what was she to think now? She wasn't going to grovel, that was for sure. If he didn't come up with reasons for what had been happening, the only conclusion she could come to was that he *was* going to get back with Tania and was going to adopt Jonathan, riding roughshod over her hopes and dreams.

'I've had the most awful indigestion for weeks,' a sixty-five-year-old woman told her some minutes later, 'and my stomach is all swollen. I don't feel ill in myself but I *am* worried.'

'Have you been seen by either of the other two doctors recently?' Andrina asked, with her glance on the woman's swollen abdomen.

'No. This is the first time I've come about it.'

'I see,' she said gravely, knowing that a lot of patients reasoned that if there was no pain, there was no problem. 'If you'll remove your lower garments and lie on the couch, I'll examine you.'

When she'd finished Andrina said, 'You can get dressed now.' When the woman was back in the chair opposite, she told her, 'It's possible that you have a problem with your ovaries, either a cyst or a tumour. I'm going to make an immediate appointment for you to see a specialist and we'll take it from there.'

The patient's colour had drained from her face.

'Do you think it might be cancer?'

'There is a possibility, yes. But there's also the chance that it could be just a non-malignant cyst. They'll soon find out and let you know one way or the other. In the meantime, try not to worry too much.'

When she'd gone Andrina thought that too many women ignored the signs of trouble, like this one had done, and when eventually they did something about it, it was too late. Hopefully it wouldn't be so on this occasion.

When she went out into Reception at the end of the morning James was chatting to Suzanne, the girl with ME, who he was now dating steadily. It was plain to see that they were madly in love and she wondered what was going to happen to his plans for working abroad once he was qualified. Was the course of true love ever smooth?

When Drew appeared he nodded briefly in her direction. Then, shrugging into his topcoat, he went out immediately to do his calls, with James following close behind.

When he came back he said briefly, 'I'm going to visit Tim Brewster after afternoon surgery. I don't know what time I'll be home. I'll eat while I'm out.'

The thought that he couldn't bear to sit at the same table as her hurt more than his cold brevity, and she just nodded and turned away.

It was half past six and Drew wasn't back. As Andrina went into the kitchen to tidy up before getting Jonathan ready for bed, there was a tap on the window. When she looked up she saw Eamon smiling at her and went to let him in.

As he perched himself on a kitchen stool, the garage owner asked, 'Where's Drew?'

She didn't really feel like chatting to Eamon. It had been a busy day and she was tense because of what was happening between Drew and herself, but he was Jonathan's godfather and someone who wasn't involved in the everlasting Tania saga.

'He's fulfilling his obligations to the Brewsters at the moment. I suppose you've heard that Tim has had a major heart attack?'

'Which once more brings him into the voluptuous Tania's orbit. She won't be complaining about that,' he remarked drily.

'They were already becoming close again before her father was taken ill,' Andrina told him flatly. 'Drew and that family have past history that isn't going to go away.'

'Maybe,' Eamon said. 'But Drew isn't going to fall for Tania's humbug again. She hurt him too much. He's a generous soul when it comes to forgiveness, but not on that scale. Drew wants to get his priorities right and they are here.' His voice had thickened and when she turned he was close behind her. 'He's a lucky guy. You wouldn't catch me neglecting you,' he breathed. Putting his arms around her, he began to lower his head towards her.

Andrina became still. He wasn't Drew. Never would be in a thousand years. Although it was comforting to be held by someone who understood her loneliness, she pushed him away before the moment became too intense.

'I'm sorry,' he groaned.

'Why?'

'Because he's the one, isn't he? Must be blind as a bat if he can't see that you're in love with him.'

'I don't show my feelings,' she told him, 'so he has no idea. And I turned on him yesterday and accused him of some pretty dreadful things. So at the moment we're not communicating at all and that's how it is likely to stay. Especially as the flame still appears to be burning between Tania and himself.'

'I might think him crazy for neglecting the baby and you,' Eamon said, his composure restored, 'but I'm sure *that* is not the case. He's just being there for the Brewsters at a time when they need him.

'Why don't you tackle him when he comes in? Get a straight answer and go on from there.' With a grin he added, 'If he doesn't feel the same way you do, tell him that there's always room for you and the little guy at my place, as long as you don't mind a few oily rags.'

When Drew got to the hospital he found Tania and Angela at Tim's bedside. Tim was still looking frail and ill, but the consultant was re-assuring.

'Mr Brewster's heart has stabilised,' he said, 'and if he continues to make good progress he may not be on the unit for too long—that is, if there are no further complications.'

'Good,' Drew told him. 'I thought that perhaps some private nursing could be organised for him when he's discharged. His wife is elderly and not very mobile.'

'By all means, if they can afford it,' the other man said. 'Very often in cases like this, the stress of caring for the sick person brings their partner to us with a similar problem.'

The two women had come to the hospital by taxi as Angela hadn't been happy for Tania to drive them in her present unreliable state. So Drew drove them home and stayed for a coffee so that he could talk to Angela about employing a nurse.

She was totally in favour of the idea and told him gratefully, 'I don't know what we would do without you, Drew.'

He patted her hand and got to his feet. Tania had said nothing, but when she came to the door with him as he was leaving she said pettishly, 'When am I going to have some of your attention?'

'You have had all you're going to get,' he said levelly. 'Just make sure that you are there *all* the time for your mother.'

As he drove back to the farm he was preparing to do what he'd been thinking about all day. He was going to make Andrina understand that he had no feelings left for Tania whatsoever and that he wanted her, Andrina, to be Jonathan's legal parent, too. When he'd convinced her of that, he would ask her to marry him and he prayed that she would say yes.

Whistler's Farm was lit up like a beacon when he got there and, knowing Andrina would most likely be in the kitchen at this time, he went round the back instead of using the front entrance.

He was smiling, buoyed up with the expectancy that soon all would be well between them again, but as he passed the window his step faltered. He drew back into the shadows, feeling as if he'd just been struck in the chest. The woman he'd been desperate to get home to was in his friend's arms.

Drew turned away and walked slowly back to the car. So much for his hopes and dreams, he thought bitterly. He'd only been there for a matter of seconds but it had been enough. He'd blown it, left it too late, he thought as he drove off mindlessly.

He'd known that Eamon was attracted to Andrina, but on the day of the christening she'd made it clear that it was one-sided and he'd even dared hope that it was because she cared for him, Drew. But what he'd just seen had put an end to those sorts of thoughts.

He needed to get a grip on himself before going back home and as the Grouse loomed up in the dark winter night he turned onto the forecourt.

It was very late when Andrina heard Drew pull up on the drive, and at that moment relief was the strongest emotion inside her. Drew was home safely from wherever he'd been. Without him she was lost. Maybe now they could talk, clear the air between them and go on from there. If he did have an explanation for the things that were worrying her, she would be only too anxious to hear it.

Eamon had said that Drew was a forgiving sort of person, and so could she be, if only he would take away the ache in her heart. But his expression when he came striding in was as cold as the air coming through the open door.

'How is Tim?' she asked with gloom descending.

'Improving.'

'That's good news, then.'

'Yes. Jonathan all right?'

'Yes. You haven't seen much of him today, have you?'

'If that was meant as a reprimand, I haven't exactly been twiddling my thumbs all day.'

'I know that,' Andrina told him with increasing dismay.

'I'm off to bed after I've looked in on him.' Without further comment he began to climb the stairs.

'We need to talk,' she said pleadingly. 'If I've offended you by what I said this morning, I really am sorry. All I ask is that you tell me what's going on. Remember, I am the stranger here. You're in your own environment, safe and secure in your own home, while I'm not. You persuaded me to come here and up to the last week or so I've felt safe, too, but if you are going to change all that with whatever is going on in the background of your life, I think I'm entitled to know.'

He'd turned and looked down at her. His eyes were still cold.

'I am weary of you doubting me, Andrina, and even if the things you accused me of *were* true, what about *your* hidden agenda that you haven't thought fit to tell me about?'

As she eyed him blankly he began to mount the stairs again, and when he reached the top he looked down at her once more and said, 'Think about it. From now on I suggest that we look after Jonathan and for the rest of it keep out of each other's way until such time as you're ready to tell me what *your* plans are.'

There was silence for a few moments after he'd disappeared from sight and she knew he would be with the child he loved so much. Then she heard his bedroom door click to and knew that the miserable day was ending in the way it had begun.

What had Drew meant about *her* having plans of her own? she wondered as she lay sleepless. The only thing occupying her mind of late had been the discovery that she'd fallen in love with the golden-haired doctor who had brought her to the Derbyshire village that was so dear to him.

There was nothing else on her agenda, except maybe an aching void because they were no longer in harmony. If she were to tell him now that she loved him he would see it as some sort of ploy, and she couldn't face having the tender shoots of her feelings trampled on.

*　　*　　*

During the days that followed Andrina felt as if there was a perpetual chill at Whistler's Farm. At the surgery she and Drew were the polite colleagues, but at home the rift was far greater, except for the times when they were seeing to Jonathan's needs.

Jonathan was the bond that bound them, Drew thought. Without him they would have nothing. There had been no further discussion about their differences and each night after Jonathan was settled he either took himself off to the Grouse or did some of the renovating work at the farm.

Breakfasts and the evening meals were strained affairs and he was beginning to wonder how much longer he could put up with what was going on between them.

He sensed that Andrina was thinner and paler of late and was puzzled. A woman in love usually bloomed, so why hadn't she? There'd been no mention or sightings of Eamon in recent days, so obviously she wasn't intending to tell *him* that she and his friend were having an affair.

While Eamon was a good godfather to their precious child, Drew didn't fancy him as a father, and if there were any further developments along that front he would inform Andrina of that fact.

It would be Christmas soon, Andrina kept thinking during the lonely evenings. Five weeks to the festive season and if ever a house needed a festive uplift, it was Whistler's Farm, because the man that she loved had withdrawn into a sombre world of his own.

As the days dragged by she wasn't the only one having jaundiced thoughts about the coming season. Drew loved Jonathan too much not to want his first Christmas to be memorable. He knew that soon he would have to put his hurt to one side and show the woman who had come so unexpectedly into his life that he still cared, no matter what.

Jonathan was changing with each day. They'd just introduced baby rice into his feeding, along with rusks and puréed meat and vegetables. The golden down on his head was thickening and he could sit up with some support. They had a contented child and in her most miserable moments Andrina was thankful that he was there, joining them together like a bridge over troubled water.

They'd noticed at the surgery that Drew wasn't his usual self. He was grim-faced and sparse of speech and very cool with Andrina, a situation between the two doctors that the staff didn't feel free to comment on.

However, Ellen Battersby was a different matter. The time when Andrina had sent her to hospital had proved to be just a cautionary measure as no damage to the retinas had been found, but the elderly villager had been impressed with the new doctor's efficiency and now always asked to see her if she had a problem.

This time it was her rheumatism that was causing her some pain and she hobbled along to the surgery to see Andrina. But her first comment after seating herself was, 'And so what's wrong with Dr Curtis these days? He looks as if he's lost a pound and found six-pence.'

'He's just very busy, that's all, Mrs Battersby,' Andrina told her, and hoped that it would satisfy her curiosity. But, of course, it didn't.

'That's what you'd like me to believe, no doubt. Not fallen out, have you?'

'No. Of course not.'

It seemed that the questions were over as she delved into the shopping bag by her side and produced a pot of home-made jam. Passing it across the desk, she said, 'Give him this from me and tell him to get on with his life.'

'Er...yes, I will,' Andrina told her, 'and thank you, Mrs Battersby.'

At the end of surgery she went into Drew's room and placed the pot of jam in front of him. For a moment the old Drew was back as he asked with a smile, 'What's that for? Are we having jam butties for lunch?'

She shook her head, pleased to see him re-laxed for once.

'It's from Ellen Battersby with her best re-gards and the advice to get on with your life.'

'Fat chance,' he said drily, as the cold mask fell into place again.

Sudden anger gripped her.

'You might be able to if you were prepared to talk to me,' she snapped.

'Yes, sure,' he said dismissively, and began writing up the notes of his last patient.

Tim Brewster was to be discharged from hospital that same day and Drew had arranged for some private nursing for him. He'd rung an agency that he'd used before and had been told that the only nurse they had available at that time was male. He'd said that was good as the patient was of the same sex and it had been arranged that Simon Standish, the male nurse, would take over Tim's care from the day he was discharged.

When Drew pulled up in front of the house that afternoon with the Brewsters, a car was parked outside their house, and as he watched a slim man of moderate height, with a mop of curly brown hair above a quirky sort of face, got out to greet them.

'I'm Simon Standish, the nurse you hired,' he said, and as a pair of twinkling brown eyes that matched the hair observed Tania huddled in the back seat of the car he added, 'Pleased to meet you all.'

As Drew drove home some time later he felt happier than he'd been in weeks. Tim was home and someone who looked as if he knew what he was doing was in charge of him. Simon seemed a pleasant fellow, but he looked as if he would stand no nonsense.

Maybe now he and Andrina could rescue their relationship. Try again, he thought.

The following day was Saturday, and when Andrina came down to breakfast Drew was giving Jonathan his cereal at the kitchen table.

He looked up quickly on hearing her soft footfalls, and she saw from his expression that he was still in a sombre mood, but it seemed that it was the surgery that he had on his mind. The short Saturday opening.

'I'll do the necessary this morning,' he said, 'to make up in part for yesterday. I am going to be around more in future, Andrina. Tim Brewster is home and I've installed a full-time nurse to take the strain off Angela.'

'Right,' she said flatly.

As Jonathan opened his mouth, waiting for the next spoonful, Drew asked, 'So, what *are* your future plans?'

She was pouring a glass of fruit juice and almost dropped the bottle.

'Why do you ask that? Is it because you sense that I'm somewhat disenchanted with you of late? Because if it is, it doesn't mean that anything has changed regarding the deal we made. When I make a commitment I keep to it and I know that you do, too. So what's the problem?'

Drew was frowning. 'I wouldn't have thought you'd need to ask. We've already discussed what we would do if one of us fell in love with another person, haven't we?'

'Yes. And? Are you saying that you want me to move out because you have plans of your own?'

'Don't be ridiculous. Jonathan needs you. It's *him* I'm thinking about.'

'It's nice to know that I'm useful for something.'

'Meaning?'

'I've felt pretty useless of late.'

He didn't take her up on that. His glance was on the clock.

'I must go. I don't want the patients waiting outside. What have you got planned for today?'

Her heart twisted. In happier times he would have said 'we', not 'you'.

He was treading on eggshells, Drew thought. If she'd arranged to be with Eamon, he would have to take a back seat.

'It may have escaped your notice,' she told him coolly, 'that it is Christmas soon and we have done no Christmas shopping for Jonathan. Shall we make a start?'

His spirits lifted. For a few hours he might be able to forget that taunting picture of Andrina in Eamon's arms. Pretend that they were a family celebrating their baby's first Christmas.

'Yes. Why not?' he agreed, his eyes brightening. 'As soon as I get back from surgery we'll go shopping.'

As they strolled amongst the crowds, with Drew pushing the pram and Andrina close by his side, she was happy. It was a bright moment in a grey existence. They were the ones who mattered, she was telling herself. The three of them. And no matter how Drew had changed, he was still the man she'd fallen in love with.

The strength and integrity that were so much a part of him hadn't disappeared, and if he thought there was happiness to be found elsewhere, who could blame him? He was the kind of man who was every woman's dream, and even if he hadn't been, he was still the answer to hers.

She wished she knew what was in his mind. He'd been so frank and open when they'd first met, but now he was like a closed book. The same didn't apply to her though. There was nothing that Drew didn't know about *her*.

He knew what she liked to eat, drink, what perfume she wore, what clothes she liked, what kind of underwear she wore if he'd ever scanned the washing line as that was the nearest he'd ever got.

He'd seen her first thing in the morning in her nightgown, without make-up, hair tousled from sleep. Seen her last thing at night, tired from the day's duties, with seduction the last thing on her mind. There was nothing mysterious or elusive for him to discover about *her*.

Although there *was* one thing he didn't know about her, and in the present climate wasn't likely to. She loved him, and always would.

'At four and a half months Jonathan is a bit young for toys,' Drew was saying, unaware of the direction that her thoughts were taking. 'What do you suggest?'

'Something that is visual and makes a noise,' she replied. 'A musical box, or baby books that play a tune, and some nice new clothes. Next year will be the one when we can go to town on toys.'

He glanced at her sharply, and she wondered if he was thinking that next year things might be very different. That one of them might have someone else to go Christmas shopping with. She wasn't to know that Drew's thoughts were going back to what he'd seen through the kitchen window on the night his hopes and plans had gone down the drain.

At that moment there was a squeal of brakes, followed by shouts of alarm, and as they swung round they saw a van careering onto the pavement behind them, scattering passers-by and coming to rest halfway through a shop window.

As shards of glass fell around them there were screams of pain and fright, and Drew turned the pram around quickly to protect Jonathan from the flying debris.

'The driver's trapped,' Andrina gasped, as they began to grasp what had happened, 'and someone inside the shop has been hurt.' But Drew didn't need telling.

He was already there beside the crashed vehicle, wrenching the door open and bending over the injured man.

The manageress of the shop had rushed onto the pavement white-faced and trembling, while inside her staff were flocking around what looked like an elderly man lying on the floor.

'Phone the emergency services,' Andrina told the dazed woman as people suffering from cuts to their faces and legs staggered around. 'Tell them we've two serious casualties and several minor ones.'

The people who'd been hurt needed all the help they could get, she thought desperately, but she couldn't leave Jonathan. As she scanned the faces of those around her, there was one that she recognised. Iris Bovey, the elderly wife of the village grocer, was standing nearby, looking dazed and bewildered but seemingly unhurt.

Andrina hurried across to her and said, 'Mrs Bovey, are you all right?'

'Yes,' she said. 'It's good to see you here, though.'

'Can I ask you to mind the baby while I go to help the injured?' She pointed to where Drew had squeezed himself into the damaged passenger seat of the van and was trying to free the driver. 'Dr Curtis is doing what he can but he needs my help.'

Which isn't going to be much, she thought, as they had no equipment with them. But there was no time to ponder that. There was the man inside the shop who appeared to have been struck by the front of the van as it had slammed through the big plate-glass window. He was still on the floor.

Still bewildered by the scale of the accident, the grocer's wife said, 'Yes. Leave the kiddie with me. I'll look after him.'

With a grateful smile Andrina watched her take hold of the handle of Jonathan's pram then she dashed into the shop.

'I'm a doctor,' she said, pushing past the shop assistants who were gathered round the man on the floor.

'We think he's dead,' one of them said as Andrina knelt beside the still form of the elderly victim. 'We didn't know what to do.'

'How long since he stopped breathing?'

'Only just.'

Even as the question was being answered she was making sure the man's tongue wasn't blocking his airway. Then she started applying cardiac compressions to the man's chest, while telling them to urge the emergency services to hurry. There was blood coming from his nose and ears, but any other injuries he might have sustained were concealed by the heavy winter overcoat he was wearing.

As she worked on him she could still hear the chaos outside and wondered how Drew was faring with the driver of the van. When she heard the wail of the ambulance sirens it was the most welcome sound she'd ever heard. It would have been difficult enough for Drew and herself to help anyone in such circumstances if they'd had their cases with them, but they'd been like the rest of the folk out there—Christmas shoppers.

As paramedics came spilling into the shop she stepped back to let them take over so that she could attend to some of the other injured. *They* were the ones who had the equipment to resuscitate the man, if it was possible.

As she looked around her Andrina could see Drew easing himself out of the driver's cab while the emergency services took over there as well. She breathed a sigh of relief. Some shopping trip it had turned out to be!

He was bloodstained and tight-lipped when she reached his side.

'I couldn't do as much as I would have liked,' he said. 'The poor guy is trapped. The fire services are on their way. They'll have to cut him free before he can be treated. But at least the paramedics can give him some pain relief. I hadn't even got the equipment to do that.'

He was glancing around him. 'Where's Jonathan?'

'I left him with Mrs Bovey. She was standing nearby and I asked her to look after him while I went to see what I could do,' she told him, as it registered that the woman and child were not where she'd left them.

'And where are they now?' he questioned.

She swallowed hard.

'I don't know. They were there…just there.'

Unease was tugging at her. She'd left their precious child with a woman she knew but only just. The Boveys were, however, Drew's patients. He'd probably known them all his life. Surely he wouldn't see anything wrong in that. Yet he wasn't exactly exuding approval.

'What was she wearing?' he asked unsmilingly.

'A beige jacket and trousers. Surely they can't be far away.'

'Iris Bovey isn't very stable these days,' he said, as his glance raked the area around them. 'She's very unpredictable and Jonathan is small and defenceless. I know that you wanted to help but he could be at risk.'

Andrina felt as if a cold hand was gripping her heart.

'How was I to know?' she cried. 'I did what seemed best.'

'Yes, I know that,' he said, 'but we're wasting time.'

Knowing that he was right, she didn't reply, just kept on scanning the busy pavements for any signs of Iris and Jonathan. When she turned to Drew he wasn't there. He'd gone across to a policeman guarding the crash scene to ask if he'd seen a woman in a beige jacket, pushing a pram.

CHAPTER EIGHT

'THERE'S a lot of those sorts of jackets about,' the officer said. 'Must be in fashion. The wife has one, but her pram-pushing days are over...I hope. What's the problem?'

'My partner and I were the first two doctors on the scene,' Drew told him urgently, 'and we've been helping the injured. Andrina asked someone from the village where we live to mind our child while we were occupied, and now the woman is nowhere to be seen. She's a patient of mine and hasn't been well lately so I'm concerned about the baby's safety.'

The policeman was serious now. 'Are you sure they're not around? Have you looked in the shops? She might have gone inside somewhere to get out of the cold.'

'I've checked them all,' Andrina gasped breathlessly as she joined them, 'and she isn't there.'

A sergeant was organising a diversion of traffic from the accident scene and the policeman called, 'Have you got a minute, Sarge?'

When he came over he said to Andrina, 'You're the doctor who was working on the injured guy in the shop, aren't you? You'll be pleased to know that they managed to resuscitate him.'

'I *am* pleased to know that,' she said worriedly, 'but I'm very concerned to find that the person I left our baby with while I was treating the man has disappeared and taken him with her.'

She felt as if there was a tight band across her chest, squeezing the life out of her. Just how confused *was* Iris Bovey?

'How long ago was this?' the officer asked.

'A quarter of an hour, twenty minutes.'

'I'll get a squad car to drive you around the area,' he said. 'One of you go with it and the other stay here in case the lady shows up.'

'Yes,' Drew said immediately, ready for action. 'I'll go. You stay here, Andrina.'

She nodded, bereft of words as she watched him hurry away with the police sergeant. Please, let Mrs Bovey bring Jonathan back safely, she begged silently of the unreliable fates.

She wouldn't have left him with just anybody. When she'd seen the grocer's wife standing nearby it had seemed the obvious thing to do if she was to help the injured, and now Drew was telling her that Iris Bovey wasn't well. Though he hadn't gone into details, she could tell that he wasn't happy about her having been left in charge of Jonathan.

As Drew sat tautly in the front seat of the squad car that had been allocated for the search, it was like looking for a needle in a haystack as his glance raked over the crowds on the pavements and down the side streets.

The woman and child could be anywhere, he thought anxiously, now that Iris had taken it into her head to leave the scene of the crash. He'd had no choice but to pass his concerns on to Andrina and he was remembering the look on her face when he'd left her there among the debris from the accident and the walking wounded who were waiting for transport to Accident and Emergency.

He knew that she loved Jonathan more than life itself. If she had been the unwitting means of bringing harm to him, their future, already uncertain, just wouldn't exist any more.

She'd done what any doctor would have done in such a situation, gone to help the injured, believing that she'd done the right thing in asking someone she knew to take care of him. It was just unfortunate that it had been a woman who'd been having some problems of her own recently.

He could cope with most things but this had him by the throat. That the person who'd always been there for Jonathan should be the means of putting him at risk didn't bear thinking about.

The police in the squad car were using the loudspeaker system in the vehicle as they drove along, giving a brief description of the woman, the baby and the pram, asking if anyone had seen them. But so far there had been no response and he wondered just how far the grocer's wife could have gone in the time.

As Andrina waited in the cold she was stopping passers-by, asking them frantically if they'd seen the woman in charge of the missing child, gasping out a description, but again there was no joy to be had.

The policeman they'd spoken to originally had left his duties at the crash scene a couple of times to see if there was any news, and she'd shaken her head tearfully.

Eventually a teenage girl stopped and said casually, 'There's a woman in the park just down the road who's dressed like that. *She's* got a baby in a pram with her.'

'Which way?' Andrina cried, and the girl pointed in the opposite direction to that the squad car had taken.

It was enough. Gathering up her long winter coat so that she didn't trip over it in her haste, Andrina was off, hope lending wings to her feet.

But as she stopped beside wrought-iron railings she saw that the small park was deserted. The dead leaves of autumn lay damp and mulchy on the paths and the bare branches of the trees stood out starkly against a sky that would soon be darkening into a winter's evening.

If it had been Iris Bovey, she'd gone, she thought achingly. She was too late. Whoever she was, she obviously hadn't lingered as it wasn't the weather for sitting in the park.

As she turned away, choking back tears, a voice spoke from behind and she swung round quickly.

'So there you are,' the grocer's wife said. 'You've been wondering where we were, I suppose. Your little one was frightened by all the screaming and shouting that was going on up there in the street so I brought him down here. But it was too cold to sit for long. We were just on our way back. Lucky we saw you.'

Andrina was only half listening. She was bending over the pram, eyes riveted on its occupant, and as if on cue Jonathan smiled his little smile and life began again.

She bent over and picked him up, cradling him to her tenderly. Observing her doubtfully, Iris said, 'I'm sorry if I've caused you any upset. You didn't think I'd run off with him, did you?'

Still speechless with relief, Andrina shook her head. She couldn't upset this elderly woman who had unwittingly caused such a panic.

Iris said, 'It was nice having him to myself for a little while. It's a long time since I pushed a pram. My husband thinks I can't do anything right these days, but I can, can't I?'

'Yes, of course you can,' Andrina told her, having found her voice. 'You've been a great help and I shall tell him so when I see him. And now shall we go and find Dr Curtis? I'm sure he's wondering where we've got to.'

It had been a fruitless search. The squad car had almost finished its circling of the surrounding area and was about to return to where it had started from when Drew saw the two women beside the park railings.

'She's found him!' he cried. 'Andrina has found Jonathan! Stop the car.'

As it came to a halt beside them, Iris backed away nervously and one of the policemen got out and went towards her. But as far as Drew was concerned, she could have flown off on a broomstick. All that concerned him was that Andrina was holding Jonathan close and he could tell from her expression that all was well.

His eyes were tender as he took them both into his arms.

'I was dreading going back there and having to tell you we hadn't found him,' he breathed, 'but wonderful woman that you are, you had it sorted. How you knew where to look I don't know, but I might have guessed that you would.'

'Mrs Bovey brought him down here because he was frightened by all the noise after the accident,' she said shakily, 'and was on her way back when she found me. A passer-by told me she'd seen someone answering her description in the park here. But when I got here the place was deserted and I was trying to cope with that when she appeared.'

'So I misjudged poor Iris,' Drew said softly. 'It's clear that she isn't as confused as I might have thought she was. Old Bovey is a bit of a tartar and maybe he makes her lose confidence in herself sometimes. Anyway, the main thing is that they're both safe and sound. We can take Jonathan home and drop Iris off at the same time.'

One of the policemen was approaching and he said, 'Are you going to press charges? The woman is adamant that she meant no harm, but the baby *was* missing for quite some time.'

Drew shook his head. 'No. It was a misunderstanding, that's all. Thanks for your help, Officer. Now that we've got our child back safely, that is all that matters. The lady is a neighbour of ours and came down here from the best of motives. We can't cause grief for someone who was doing us a favour.'

'Fair enough,' the officer agreed, and as the squad car drove off into the gathering dusk Drew said to Iris, 'We'll take you home, Mrs Bovey, and thanks for taking care of Jonathan.'

As they drove away they were all silent. After those euphoric moments when he'd found them beside the park Drew had said little and now, with darkness upon them and all thoughts of Christmas shopping forgotten, they were both anxious to get home to some welcoming warmth.

Their elderly passenger had nodded off as soon as the car had left the town centre and was now snoring gently.

Every time Drew looked at Jonathan, safe in his baby seat in the back of the car, he smiled, but the smiles were all directed at the child, she noticed, and thought that now he had calmed down he was still remembering how she'd left the baby with a woman that she hardly knew. It was something that *she* wasn't going to forget either, but what should she have done? Given Iris a medical examination before she'd passed Jonathan over to her?

No. But maybe she should have given the situation more thought before dashing off. Yet she wouldn't have been able to start CPR on the injured man if she'd been any longer in getting to his side, and by the time the paramedics had come, it would have been too late.

Closing her eyes, she leaned back in the car seat. Nothing was going right between Drew and herself at the moment, she thought wearily. It was as if those blissful first weeks with him at the farm had never happened.

Tania's demands had been irksome enough then, but in recent weeks he'd had *all* the Brewsters on his mind and she'd been lagging far behind on his list of priorities. But today she'd thought that they were getting closer again and then Jonathan had disappeared.

There would have been none of this uncertainty if she'd fallen in love with Eamon, she thought wryly. He would be there if she lifted a finger, but she didn't want Drew's friend. She wanted the man himself.

Casting a quick glance in her direction, Drew was aware of her pallor and exhaustion. He wanted to stop the car, take her into his arms and cuddle and kiss the spirit back into her. But their relationship was changing all the time and there was nothing a woman liked less than to be in the arms of one man when she wanted to be in those of another.

He knew that he should be bringing up the matter of Eamon and what he'd seen through the kitchen window, but once it was out in the open it might propel Andrina into making a decision sooner than she would have done, and every moment they were together at the farm was too precious to squander.

He hoped that his friend wasn't treating what was going on between Andrina and himself as a quick flirtation. Eamon would have him to answer to if he was *and* he would have to convince him that he was a fit person to take care of Jonathan on a permanent basis.

Because his doubts about that had already surfaced. But he kept telling himself that he need have no worries on that score as *he* would be there on the sidelines all the time and if either of them put a foot wrong...

He groaned inwardly. What was he thinking of? If Andrina heard that, she would conclude that he was blaming her for leaving Jonathan as she had, when he knew full well it had to be a matter of life and death for her to have done such a thing. And as for the rest of it, she loved the baby too much to ever let a guy like Eamon near him unless she was sure of his worth.

But she *had* been in Eamon's arms, and he knew from past experience that she didn't spread her favours around lightly.

When they stopped outside the grocer's the shop was shut but the lights were still on, and when Drew tapped on the door the man himself came to open it.

'We've brought Iris home from the town centre,' Drew told him. 'She's had a stressful afternoon and is ready for a cup of tea.'

'Is that so?' he grunted. 'She can make me one while she's at it.'

'So much for hoping he would take the hint,' Andrina said as they drove off. 'Maybe you're right. That Iris would be better with less bossing around from her husband.'

Andrina was shivering when she got out of the car and Drew said, 'You're suffering from delayed shock. Go straight to bed and I'll bring you some hot, sweet tea up once I've got Jonathan settled.'

She shook her head. Her glance was on the baby in his arms.

'I can't bear to let him out of my sight.'

He nodded.

'I know. But do as I say and I'll bring him up to you. He can snuggle down beside you.'

'All right,' she agreed wearily as they went inside, but with her foot on the bottom stair she turned, 'I really am sorry for what I did.'

He was moving towards the kitchen to put the kettle on and didn't register the pleading in her eyes.

'Forget it,' he said briskly. 'You weren't to know that Iris Bovey is having behaviour problems. The incident is over. No harm done.'

No harm done! she thought grimly. Was he kidding? She could tell a mile off that he wasn't feeling as relaxed about it as he would have her believe. It would be all the more reason to keep her on the edge of things.

Drew took her the drink and brought the baby to her, as he'd promised, and when he looked in on them later they were both asleep, with Andrina holding him close.

What could he do to end the day on a brighter note? he wondered. If the local garden centre was still open he could get a tree and ornaments and have it up by the time she woke up.

He got there with just minutes to spare, made his purchase and then it was back home and all systems go. When Andrina came down later, it was there in all its brightness. A sign of the fast-approaching season. A large spruce decorated with gold and silver balls and coloured lights, emblazoning a corner of the farmhouse's spacious sitting room on this their first

Christmas together. Whether it would also be their last he had yet to find out, but for the moment he was putting the thought to the back of his mind.

He was seated by the fire, flipping through a medical journal, when she appeared huddled inside a warm robe. When he looked up he saw tears and was on his feet in an instant.

'What's wrong?'

'Nothing,' she sobbed. 'I was remembering the awful feeling inside me when we didn't know what had happened to Jonathan.'

He held out his arms.

'Come here,' he said softly, and she obeyed.

As he cradled her to him he murmured, 'I know what you mean. But he's here with us where he belongs, snug and safe in his cot. So cheer up and tell me if you like the tree.'

A smile was replacing the tears as she looked up at him.

'Yes, of course I do. It's lovely. Where did you manage to get it at this time of night?'

'Just caught the garden centre before they closed. Are you ready for something to eat? You must be famished.'

She nodded but didn't move out of his arms and he said gently, 'Should we be doing this under the circumstances? I don't want you to think that the moment I touch you I'm ready to take it from there. I think that we both know there is a reason why I shouldn't.'

'I'm sorry,' she said stiffly, and this time she took the hint and moved out of his hold. 'I rely on you too much.'

Drew gave a twisted smile.

'Maybe, but it won't always be like that,' he reminded her, with Eamon in mind.

'It won't have to be, will it?' she said, misunderstanding completely, and moved towards the kitchen.

Sunday was a much more tranquil day than Saturday had been. Marion came round in the afternoon and said she'd been told they'd been treating the injured at an accident in the town the day before and wanted to know all about it.

'Ask Drew,' Andrina said. 'I still can't bear to think about it.'

'Why? Was it so bad?' she asked.

'It was bad enough. We were told afterwards that the brakes of the van had failed. It came careering onto the pavement and smashed through a shop window. The fire services had to cut the driver free, and when Drew rang last night to enquire about him he was told that he was in Intensive Care with chest injuries and multiple fractures. The other seriously injured person was an elderly man who was standing in the shop near the window. The van hit him full on and he suffered a cardiac arrest.'

'Yes, but you'll have seen that kind of thing before surely?'

'I have. The reason I don't want to look back on it is because we lost Jonathan.'

Marion's mouth had gone slack with amazement.

'Lost him!' she said incredulously. 'How?'

'Andrina asked Iris Bovey to look after him while she went to help the man, and when we'd done our bit and went to get him, both he and Iris had gone.'

'Gone where?'

'Exactly. That is what we didn't know.'

'Oh, dear, and because Iris hasn't been herself lately, you thought the worst?'

'Something like that, but it turned out that she'd taken him into a nearby park because of all the noise and commotion at the crash scene. So all was well that ended well,' he said equably. Observing his expression, Andrina wondered if that was really how he saw it in the cold light of day.

'You poor things,' Marion said sympathetically. 'You must have been frantic.'

'Yes, we were,' he said in the same measured tone. 'It was one of those moments when parenting and doctoring clashed, but Andrina found him, thank goodness, and we managed to convince Iris that she'd done the right thing, so she was none the wiser regarding the panic she'd caused. She's a nice woman who's short of a bit of tender loving care.'

'And so with that traumatic incident in the past, what are you planning for the baby's first Christmas?' the elderly receptionist asked.

'I thought we'd have a party on Christmas Eve,' Drew said before Andrina could reply. 'Would you be free to come, Marion? It would be nice to have Jonathan's godparents there.'

'Yes. I'm free on Christmas Eve.' She beamed. 'What about Eamon?'

'He hasn't been asked yet but I'm sure there won't be a problem,' he said smoothly, telling himself he must be crazy. Stage-managing the event so that Andrina could be with Eamon. Throwing them together when he was wishing his friend miles away.

Andrina didn't comment. The last thing she wanted was a house full of people on Christmas Eve. She wanted it to be just the three of them as they hung up a Christmas stocking for Jonathan and spread their presents beneath the tree, but maybe Drew was thinking there was safety in numbers.

She suspected that he was inviting Eamon so that she wouldn't feel left out. Drew didn't know that the less she saw of the garage owner, the better.

*　　*　　*

In the week before Christmas they decided that they would do any future festive shopping separately after that disastrous first attempt, with Andrina doing the food shopping one evening and Drew taking advantage of late-night opening in town to do the rest.

Drew had known for weeks what he would like to give Andrina, a ring of the kind that would tell the world they belonged together, but the Eamon episode had put paid to that and he was having to have a rethink.

On Andrina's part, one afternoon when Drew was out on calls she'd taken Jonathan with her to a professional photographer to have a studio portrait taken of them to give to him on Christmas morning. She thought ruefully as she posed for it with the baby on her knee that in time to come it would be something to remember her by...should he want to.

In those last few days before Christmas the thing that both children and adults always hoped might happen did come to pass. It began to snow. Not just a fine white sprinkling but heavy flakes that stuck purposefully wherever they fell.

It came in the evening out of a leaden sky, and as they watched it fall onto the trees and lawns at the front of the house Drew said whimsically, 'It might look like winter wonderland out there, but if it keeps it up we're going to have trouble visiting patients in the more remote areas.'

Jonathan had just had his bath and was wrapped in a big towel as Andrina held him up to see the swirling white flakes.

'Just wait until you and I are out there, making a snowman,' he said to the baby, and Andrina winced. There'd been no mention of her at all.

The snow fell steadily through the early hours of the night and when she looked out of her bedroom window the next morning it was sparkling like diamonds beneath a winter sun.

She caught her breath. It was a beautiful sight and so easy to forget that it had its down side when roads were blocked and blizzards whistled across the moors above the village.

When he'd eaten Drew went out to clear the drive so that they could get to Monday morning surgery, and while he was out there she dressed Jonathan in his warmest clothes and thought about the day ahead.

Although the flu outbreak had slackened off there were still lots of people with coughs and colds coming to the surgery because remedies from the chemist weren't helping and antibiotics were needed.

They'd been called out to one or two cases of hypothermia among the elderly during the past week, and as the voice of the morning weather forecaster butted into her thoughts she wondered what sort of a day it was going to be…

It seemed that there was going to be more heavy snow, but this time not a still white carpet to admire. Gale-force winds were being forecast during the next twenty-four hours, which would cause blizzard conditions in exposed areas, and she thought that maybe the people around the Pennines were going to have to pay a price for a white Christmas.

James was off sick with a gastric bug and so she was going to take the late surgery while Drew did the house calls, and when they dropped Jonathan off at the nursery they explained to Serena that one of them would pick him up at the first opportunity.

'Fine,' she said and as they turned to go, 'Are you going to the hunt ball, by any chance? I'm selling tickets.'

'Yes. I think so,' Drew told her. 'Save me a couple, will you?'

'It's the top social event in the area, and takes place on New Year's Eve,' he said as they went out to their cars.

Andrina nodded. She recalled Tania mentioning it when she'd barged into the farm that first time, using it as an excuse to talk to Drew. Since then *she'd* never given it a thought, but it would seem that someone else had.

'If I go, it will be with Eamon,' she said smoothly, cringing at the idea that Drew might think she was expecting him to take her. As the lie hung between them she saw that he was nodding as if he wasn't surprised.

He had some cheek, she thought angrily. All right, she'd lied, but what if she had? He was making it just a bit too obvious that he was happy to be unloading her onto his friend.

And what was she going to do now? Ask Eamon to take her to the most salubrious occasion of the calendar year, like some forgotten Cinderella, when she'd been at such pains to fight him off? Why couldn't she have just said that she wasn't going?

There was a hospital report on her desk when she got to the surgery. It was about the woman that she'd suspected might have ovarian cancer and her face was sombre as she picked it up. But as she began to read her brow cleared. The problem had been a cyst, not a tumour, and it wasn't malignant. Ovarian cysts usually weren't, but there was always the chance that one might be.

When she'd finished reading the report she sat back for a moment. After that unsettling conversation at the nursery she'd needed some brightness to start off the day and that had been it.

If she went to the ball she would have to do some clothes shopping, she thought as the day wore on. There was no way the flame silk dress was going to put in another appearance. That was *if* Eamon was prepared to be picked up and put down when it suited her.

She was still cringing at the thought of what she'd done and had decided that she would ask the favour of him over the phone. It would be easier that way. He wouldn't be able to see the mortification on her face.

But to her surprise and dismay he appeared when she was having a quick bite in her room before afternoon surgery.

'Drew around?' he asked casually.

She shook her head.

'No. He's out on his calls.'

'Any joy between the two of you?' he asked in the same easy tone.

'Why do you ask?'

'Well, if he still hasn't come up to scratch, how do you fancy tripping the light fantastic with me at the hunt ball.'

'Yes,' she said immediately, unable to believe her luck.

He smiled.

'Oops! That was fast. Do I take it that you've had a change of heart?'

She shook her head again.

'No. I don't want you to get the wrong idea. Drew has bought two tickets but I don't know for certain who he's taking, so I either stay at home or accept your kind invitation.'

'So I'm still second best, am I?'

'I'm afraid so. If you want to take back the offer, I'll understand.'

'Naw, it stays. I'll get the tickets, then.' Before she could say anything further, he loped off and left her to finish her lunch in peace.

As the afternoon wore on the weather worsened. Was this what old Eli had forecast? she wondered with an uneasy feeling. The kind of conditions that brought the power lines down and those living on the tops were snowed in? It was only a couple of hours since all had been white, still and sparkling.

Where was Drew? she wondered. Hopefully he was on his way back to the practice. He knew the roads and lanes like the back of his hand. If anyone was unlikely to get lost in a snowstorm it was he, but she was anxious to see him back nevertheless.

Sometimes they brought just one car to the surgery and on other occasions, if there was a chance that Andrina might be needed to do some visits, they brought both. Today, with James being absent, they'd brought them both, in case an emergency came up.

In the middle of afternoon surgery she rang Drew's mobile and was relieved when he answered immediately.

'I'm running a bit late,' he said. 'Driving conditions are not good. The roads are treacherous. Are there many for the late surgery?'

'No,' she told him. 'I think the weather is keeping them away. As soon as I've seen those who are here, I'm going to pick Jonathan up and go home.'

'Yes, do,' he agreed. 'I'll call at the practice to clear away before I come back to the farm.

Any news on James? Do you think I should go and check him over?'

'It's up to you, but do, please, be careful. Don't get bogged down in a drift on any of those lonely tracks. From what I've been told, the Snake Pass gets blocked very quickly, and locally the narrow lanes become undrivable even faster.'

'I'll remember that,' he said meekly. 'I *have* been out in bad weather before, you know.' She could tell that he was smiling.

It was as the last patient was leaving and the staff were anxious to do likewise that a call came through and it was Marion who answered it.

'It's Eli Thompson from up by the reservoirs,' she said. 'He's coughing and gasping. Sounds as if he's ready to draw his last breath. He's asking for Dr Curtis to go and visit him. Shall I see if I can get him on his mobile?'

Andrina hesitated. In another hour the call would have been transferred to the call-out service that covered evenings and weekends, but at this time of the afternoon the responsibility was theirs.

'Yes, try him,' she said. 'I spoke to him earlier and he said he was on his way back, but I don't know exactly where he was.'

'No answer,' Marion reported seconds later.

Andrina nodded. 'He'll be out of reach of the signal somewhere. I'll have to go.'

'It's time Eli was in care, but try telling him.' Marion said. 'Can't we just send for an ambulance? I don't like to think of you driving along that dark road.'

'We can't send for an ambulance until I've seen him,' she said. 'I'll take oxygen with me and some medication for his chest, as there is no way he'll be able to get to a chemist in this and they won't want to come out to deliver a prescription either in these conditions.'

As she buttoned up her coat and reached for her bag she was thinking that it was only minutes since he'd been in her thoughts and now she was about to meet the elderly Romeo.

CHAPTER NINE

ON HIS way back to the practice Drew called at the Brewsters' house. He hadn't seen Tim in the last few days and as his GP felt that he owed him a visit.

Simon Standish, the male nurse that he had engaged to take care of him, had rung him a couple of times with progress reports and now he was about to see for himself how his elderly patient was recovering.

It wasn't going to be a prolonged call as the weather was getting steadily worse, which was one of the reasons why he was stopping off— in case the Brewsters became snowed in on the lane where theirs was the only house.

He found Tim still improving, and the atmosphere in the household calm and organised, with Angela content to see her husband being cared for and, amazingly, Tania less strident. She was more amenable in word and deed and, where at one time she would have fastened onto him like a leech, he got the impression that she was only mildly pleased to see him.

When he was leaving the nurse came to the door with him, and when Drew remarked on the change in his ex-wife Simon smiled.

'I made it clear from the start that I wouldn't put up with any tantrums. I've met her type before. I told Tania that she had to pull her weight, no sulks or aggravation for her parents, and she appears to have taken note of what I said.'

Drew smiled.

'You seem to be just the right sort of person to cope with her.'

Simon grinned back at him. 'There are more ways of nursing than giving medicine. Tim Brewster needs tranquillity if he is to get well again, and with a petulant hothouse flower like his daughter around it would have been in short supply if she hadn't changed her ways. She was a challenge that I couldn't resist, but I'm only tough with her for her own good.'

As he was pulling out of the Brewsters' drive Drew's mobile rang and he stopped the car. It was Marion, sounding anxious.

'We had a call from Eli Thompson a few minutes ago,' she said. 'He was having breathing problems. I tried to get hold of you but you must have been out of range.'

'I'll go there now,' he said.

'Dr Bell has already gone. That's why I'm ringing you. I'm worried about her. The road that leads to the reservoirs is so dark and what the winds will be like out there I shudder to think. It's so open. The snow is beginning to drift here so it will really be piling up around that area.'

'I'm on my way,' he said briefly. 'Who's going to pick Jonathan up?'

'I am. I'll take him to my place until one of you shows up.'

'Fine.' And with nerve ends tightening he went to track down Andrina.

This had been a mistake, Andrina was thinking as she came out of Eli's cottage into the wild night. It had been difficult enough getting there, and while she'd been inside it had got worse. She should have done as Marion had suggested and got an ambulance out there without embarking on the nightmare ride herself. As a much heavier vehicle than her small car, it wouldn't have been at so much risk.

The old man had calmed down when she'd got there but he was still wheezing heavily, which wasn't surprising with the woodsmoke from the fire and tobacco smoke from a battered clay pipe polluting the air.

The oxygen had brought immediate relief and after showing him how to use it she'd produced the antibiotics she'd taken with her.

'Your tubes are not in very good shape,' she'd told him chidingly.

'What do you expect at my age?' he'd croaked.

It hadn't been the moment to point out that not smoking and trying coal on his fire instead of wood might help, so she'd told him, 'I want you to be cared for over Christmas. I'm going to phone for an ambulance. The weather is dreadful out there and it might take it some time to get here, but it is what you need. They will either keep you in hospital or find you a temporary place in a care home.' As he'd opened his mouth to protest she added, 'Please, don't argue. It will be just for over the holidays and until your chest clears.'

'Why didn't young Drew come to see me instead of you?' he'd grumbled.

'He will be saying the same thing,' she'd told him. 'And now I've got to get going before I'm snowed in here.'

As she drove slowly along the narrow lane that led away from the cottage Andrina was acutely conscious of the dark still waters to one side of the track.

With headlamps full on she could see that there was quite a drop to the water, with a low metal barrier separating it from the road. In daylight it was a picturesque spot but not tonight. She was only minutes away from the village, yet it felt as if she was in no man's land.

At the end of the track was the road, and once she was on it she would feel safe. The gritters had been out and conditions there would be much better. But first she had to get there.

As the car slithered and crunched on the snow, veering from side to side in the darkness, and the waters of the reservoir glittered up at her, her hands were so tight on the steering-wheel her veins were bulging.

Suddenly it happened, the thing she'd been dreading. She lost control of the car on a particularly icy part of the track and went through the barrier.

She waited for it to plunge into the cold waters but it came to a halt, and as it teetered on the edge of the drop she was flung forward. Her head hit the steering-wheel and she knew no more.

As Drew turned off the road onto the track that led to Eli's cottage he saw headlamps ahead of him and thought that it must be Andrina on her way back. No one else would have cause to be driving along there in such weather. But in the same second he realised the lights weren't moving and they weren't pointing towards him either. They were shining across the water, which was ominous.

With dread engulfing him, he drove on, and when he saw the outline of the car hanging over the edge of the drop his insides turned over. He was out of his own vehicle in a flash, and as he ran round to the driver's side he saw Andrina slumped over the wheel.

His first thought was to get her out, but supposing the movement sent the car into the water and her with it before he'd had the chance to free her? That would be catastrophic.

He had to get help, and fast, but first he checked her pulse and was relieved to find its beat reassuring. She was making no movement while unconscious, but he reasoned if she came round and moved it could send the car over the edge.

He phoned the emergency services and was told that there was an ambulance already on its way to Eli Thompson's.

'How long is it going to be?' he asked tightly. 'I have a car here ready to topple into the reservoir and my colleague is inside it, unconscious.'

'A good ten minutes. It set off a quarter of an hour ago, but road conditions are grim. Sounds as if you might need the fire services as well,' the emergency operator said.

'Yes, I know that,' he said abruptly, 'but, please, radio the ambulance and tell them that we need them first.'

He was assuming that Andrina had hit her head as the car had jolted forward. Her seat belt had prevented her from going through the windscreen, otherwise she would have been in the water before he'd got there, so she must have hit the steering-wheel.

As he was bending over her she groaned and opened her eyes, and he said urgently, 'Don't move, Andrina. The car is hanging over the edge of the reservoir.'

She looked at him blearily and he knew that what he'd said hadn't registered.

'Why are *you* here?' she asked in a slurred voice. 'I've sorted Eli out and sent for an ambulance.'

He nodded. 'Good girl. Now, what I want you to do is stay very still. I'm going to get in the back of the car to balance it more evenly and we're going to stay like that until help arrives. If we both end up in the water at these temperatures, Jonathan could be an orphan twice over.'

There was no answer. She was slumped back in the seat this time, eyes closed and head lolling.

It wasn't too long before the ambulance came pushing its way through the snow towards them, but it seemed like an eternity. When two paramedics peered through the window of the car, he urged them, 'Get my colleague out first.'

'It might go over with you in it if we do,' they told him. 'We need some more weight at the back here while we lift her out.'

'Just do it,' he urged. 'Her safety is all I care about.'

'Hello, there,' a voice called from behind, and a fireman appeared from the whirling flakes, but there was no sound of the vehicle that had brought him there.

'We can't get the appliance up here it's too narrow,' he said, taking in the situation immediately, 'but if we three put our weight on the back to level the car, you can get out of the back seat and lift her out.'

It worked, and as two more members of the fire crew appeared at that moment, carrying loose rocks to prop up the car, the paramedics stretchered Andrina to the ambulance.

'What about the old fellow that we came to pick up?' one of them asked. 'How much further is it to his place? If we leave it much longer, we mightn't be able to get to him.'

'Just down the road there,' Drew told them, his glance on Andrina's white face. 'He's in his nineties and has developed bronchial problems.'

'Fine,' one said, and as the firemen lumbered off, having told Drew that they would come back in daylight hours now that the car was safe, they went to collect Eli.

There were a few protests when they got to the cottage, but Drew was in no mood for delays, and as soon as the old man had put some tobacco and a clean pair of long johns in a plastic carrier bag, they were off.

If he hadn't gone to the Brewsters' this would never have happened, Drew thought dismally as he waited for Andrina to come back from X-ray. Or at least it would have been he whose life had been at risk, not that of the woman who had given new meaning to his days. If he'd gone straight back to the surgery he would have been in time to take Eli's call and go out there himself.

The old fellow had been admitted to a geriatric ward and was waiting to see the doctor, and Drew couldn't help thinking that this was the best place for him over the Christmas holiday. He would have food and warmth…and company.

'No damage done,' the doctor in Accident and Emergency told them when he'd examined Andrina's X-ray. 'There'll be lots of bruising, but you'll do. We're going to keep you in for a couple of days to check for concussion, but we should have you home for Christmas.'

Andrina had become fully conscious in the ambulance and her first thoughts had been for the baby.

'Jonathan?' she'd asked tearfully. 'What about *him*?'

'I've rang Marion and explained what has happened,' Drew had told her, 'and she's going to keep him with her for the time being.'

She'd turned away to stare bleakly at the darkened windows of the ambulance. Some Christmas this was going to be.

And now the doctor in A and E was telling her that she was to be kept in for observation. Was anything ever going to go right for them? she wondered.

They put her in a small side ward and the moment she was settled she urged Drew to go and see to Jonathan.

'I don't want to leave you,' he said.

It was true. He would relive those moments beside the reservoir for the rest of his days, but he knew that Jonathan came top of her list of priorities. He wasn't sure what *his* position was. Tagging on after Eamon most likely.

Andrina smiled for the first time since he'd found her.

'I'll be all right. Just go and take him home. I won't be expecting you back. You'll have enough to do, feeding him and putting him to bed.'

'I could come back afterwards. Marion would come round, I'm sure.'

'Not in this weather. Thank you for coming to find me, Drew. Though I didn't know anything about it at the time, which perhaps was fortunate. I thought I was going into the water, you know.'

'Yes, well, you didn't, did you?' he said quietly, as he digested the fact that he'd just been told to stay away. 'Do you want Eamon to come and see you?'

'Eamon? No.' She wasn't giving anything away. 'I'm tired and my head hurts. I'm going to try to sleep when you've gone.' With a catch in her voice she added, 'Just two days to Christmas and I'm stuck in here.'

'Does it matter?' he asked sombrely.

'Yes, of course it does. It's Jonathan's first Christmas.'

'You could have been drowned out there. *That* would have mattered. There will be other Christmas-times for Jonathan and he'll need you then.'

'*And* you. He needs you just as much as he needs me.'

'Yes, well, we'll have to see, won't we?'

He was preparing her, she thought, conditioning her for what was to come. She still had the feeling that Tania had been forgiven, but without taking him up on what he'd said she closed her eyes, and when she opened them a few seconds later he'd gone.

He could understand Andrina being worried about Jonathan after what had happened, Drew thought as he began to sort out the Christmas decorations after putting the baby to bed, but she could have been killed. Mercifully she hadn't been and he'd been sending up prayers of thankfulness ever since. But someone had to get ready for Christmas and he was the only one to do it.

He'd reluctantly rung Eamon and told him what had happened and he'd been eager to go and see her, but Drew had explained that Andrina had said she wanted to be left alone and he'd agreed to stay put.

Drew wasn't to know that ever since she'd been so willing to go to the hunt ball with him Eamon had started to hope again, even though he knew he was only second best.

Drew was debating whether to cancel the party they'd arranged for Christmas Eve. It was only two days off, and with Andrina in hospital there would be no point to it, unless she came home by then...and felt up to it.

He went to see her in the lunch-hour between surgeries the next day, and the moment he appeared beside the bed she asked, 'How is Jonathan?'

He smiled. 'How did I know that would be the first thing you'd say? He's fine. Said he would have come with me but he had a date with Serena.'

She smiled back, but it was more of a grimace as her head was still tender from the bump of the previous day.

'The doctor has been to see me,' she told him, 'and he says I can go home in the morning. I'll get a taxi so that you don't have to leave morning surgery.'

'I will pick you up,' he said firmly. 'Forget the taxi. James can manage on his own for a little while.'

'All right. Whatever you say,' she agreed meekly.

There was still the feeling of listlessness in her, as if all her hopes and dreams were slowing down into nothing.

'I think we should cancel the party on Christmas Eve,' he told her, and that brought a reaction.

She shook her head.

'No. Let's keep to the arrangements. It's not as if we're planning a state banquet. I need some company after yesterday's events.'

It wasn't true. She needed *him*...and Jonathan. No one else. But he wasn't to know that because she kept putting off telling him that she loved him in case it all fell apart even more.

'All right,' he said flatly, thinking she was desperate to see Eamon. 'The party is on. I've got all tomorrow to get ready for it. Now I have to go. I wish I didn't, but I've still got some home visits to do.'

'Eli came in to see me this morning,' she said, wanting to keep him by her side.

'How is he?'

'Still wheezing but on the mend. Having had a good breakfast and a nice meal last night, he's beginning to think that Christmas won't be so bad.'

'That's good. I'll pop in to see him before I leave.'

'He'll like that. He wanted to know where you were when I got to his cottage.'

He laughed, and bent and kissed her bruised cheek gently. 'Take care until I get you back home, Andrina.'

'Yes, sure,' she said easily, and thought *that* situation might occur sooner than he was expecting if she could use some persuasion on the medical staff. If it *was* going to be their first and last Christmas together, she was going to make every moment count. Her apathy had gone. She was feeling positive for the first time in days.

Early that evening Andrina spoke to the ward sister and asked if she could go home.

'I have a young baby at home. It's his first Christmas and we have much to do before Christmas morning. I feel all right now, and the doctor did say I could go in the morning.'

'I'll have a word with him,' she said with an understanding smile. 'That's if I can find him. He might have gone off duty.'

The nurse came back a few moments later and the smile was still there.

'He was still around and, yes, he says you can go. But no exertion, and if you start to feel ill or have any severe head pains you get back to us immediately. And we want you back in Outpatients on January the second.'

'Yes, sure,' she agreed.

When the nurse asked if she should ring Drew to come for her, Andrina told her that he would have had a very busy day and she didn't want to bother him but she would be obliged if she would ring for a taxi.

Andrina was smiling as she put her key in the lock. At least part of her world was righting itself. She was back home with those she loved. In a matter of seconds she would see Jonathan. He would be asleep at this time but just to look down at him would be enough.

As the door swung back her jaw went slack. She'd been assuming too much. The baby wasn't in bed. He was in Tania's arms, smiling up at her in the cluttered hall that was full of holly, mistletoe and packages.

That was the first thing her astonished gaze took in. The second was Drew, smiling and relaxed, coming through the door that led to the kitchen with two glasses of wine.

When he saw her he almost dropped them.

'Andrina! This *is* a surprise!' he said, putting the glasses down on the hall table. 'I thought you weren't due home until tomorrow.'

'So it would seem,' she said drily as she went up to Tania and held out her arms for the baby.

As the other woman handed him over she smirked. 'Yes, you *are* full of surprises, aren't you, Andrina? But, then, so am I, aren't I, Drew?'

Ignoring the comment, Andrina turned to Drew. 'What is Jonathan doing up at this hour? I thought we had a routine.'

'It's only a quarter to nine,' he said levelly. 'He has been to bed once but I think his teeth are bothering him. The first one is almost through.'

'Yes, I *do* know that,' she snapped. 'I *have* only been away from him since yesterday.'

She was being unreasonable and knew it, picking on him because her homecoming had fallen flat. He sighed and that made her feel even more disgruntled.

'Tania stopped by to tell me the latest news,' he said in the same even tone.

'You don't have to explain yourself to me,' she told him coolly. 'It's *your* house, *your* practice.' She looked down at the child in her arms. '*Your* blood relative.'

'I'll be going, then,' Tania said smoothly. 'Bye for now, Drew, darling.' She sauntered out into the night, leaving them to silence.

When she'd gone Andrina went into the sitting room and slumped down onto the couch with Jonathan still in her arms. She'd been like a nagging wife out there, she was thinking when he appeared in the doorway.

'What was all that about?' he asked levelly. 'And why didn't you ring and ask me to come for you?'

'I butted into your cosy evening, didn't I?'

'Are you sure that you're not still suffering from the blow to your head?'

That was the last straw. She got to her feet.

'I'll settle Jonathan and then I'm going to bed. You shouldn't have let Tania go. You could have carried on where you left off.'

Before she'd even got to the top of the stairs Andrina was overcome with contrition. She'd just made a fool of herself, been objectionable to both Drew and his ex-wife, and all because the sight of Jonathan in the other woman's arms and the smile on Drew's face when he'd appeared with the wine had made her realise just how much her world was crumbling.

She turned, about to make her peace with him, but before she could do so she heard the front door slam. Seconds later his car drove off into the night and it wasn't hard to guess where he'd gone.

As Drew drove to pick up the turkey he'd ordered from a farm higher up the hillside he was thinking that he should have told Andrina where he was going, but he'd let her rile him

and he shouldn't have done. She'd had a
dreadful few days and could be excused for
being edgy. He wasn't going to be out long
and when he got back he would put things
right.

When she'd walked through the front door
it had taken him all his time not to rush forward and take her in his arms, but her expression had put an end to that sort of impulse. He
knew that she had reservations about Tania
and couldn't blame her for that as the other
woman was never civil to her when they met,
and to find her holding Jonathan after Andrina
had been fretting to get back to him was certain to be something she could have done without.

When he collected the turkey the farmer
wanted to talk, but after thanking him and pay-
ing for the bird Drew was off, eager to salvage
what was left of the evening if Andrina wasn't
already asleep.

It seemed that she was. He called her name
softly several times outside her bedroom door,
but there was no response and in the end he

went back downstairs and finished putting up the holly and mistletoe.

The party was a success, though not from any high spirits on her part, Andrina thought guilt-ily as they cleared away afterwards. Eamon had been very attentive, which had made her feel edgy, and Drew had been the opposite, quiet and withdrawn with her but pleasant and welcoming with the other guests, who had in-cluded most of the staff from the practice, Mr and Mrs Bovey, the vicar and Tom Blair, the owner of the Home Farm who had consulted Andrina about the embarrassing rash. He'd never been back so she supposed the cream had done the trick. Careful as he was with pes-ticides, he would have to be even more careful with them in the future.

In the middle of it all Jonathan had woken up. His teeth had been bothering him again and as Andrina had hushed him back to sleep in the quiet nursery she'd wanted to stay there, away from Eamon's attentions and Drew's lack of them.

'What's wrong?' he asked from the doorway as she crooned softly to the restless baby, and she thought that he had a built-in radar where Jonathan was concerned, but with herself it was as if he never tuned in to *her* needs and aspirations.

'It's his teeth again,' she said softly as the baby's eyelids began to droop. 'The sooner they put in an appearance the better.' And she laid him gently back in the cot.

'How do you think it's going?' Drew asked as she straightened the covers.

'Fine. Our guests are making up for our lack of zest.'

He nodded. 'Maybe on my part, but you have Eamon to entertain you.'

'Yes,' she agreed absently, and wondered what Drew would say if he knew it was because she'd shown so much false enthusiasm when Eamon had asked her to go to the ball with him.

'I haven't wished you a merry Christmas,' Drew said in a low voice as she was about to go back to their guests.

'That's all right,' she said flatly. 'You don't have to. It isn't part of the package.'

He took her arm and drew her towards him and she didn't resist.

'Those of us on the sidelines have to gather up the crumbs when we can,' he said with his mouth almost touching hers. His kiss was light and undemanding until she put her arms around his neck and kissed him back, and then it changed into a hungry wave of desire that had them clinging to each other as if they would never let go.

It was Marion's voice calling up to them, asking if everything was all right, that brought them down to earth, and as they separated Andrina wiped her hand across her lips. Drew saw the movement in the darkened nursery and his mouth twisted as he thought that she'd let him kiss her on sufferance, and as she led the way downstairs he followed her in silence.

The highlight of the evening as far as the rest of those present were concerned came when James announced his engagement to Suzanne, and that seemed to set the tone. It was a moment for congratulations and popping champagne corks but, delighted though she was at their news, Andrina was envious. Why was it always someone else who was in that state of bliss? She'd found her soul mate, but *he* was on a different wavelength.

She hadn't yet apologised to Drew for her tetchiness the previous night when she'd come home from hospital because she thought he'd slammed out of the house to catch up with Tania. She'd fallen into a miserable, troubled sleep the moment her head had touched the pillow and so hadn't seen him come back with the turkey and hadn't been aware that he'd only been gone a matter of minutes.

Conversation had been in short supply since and every time their eyes met she looked away. What Christmas Day was going to be like she didn't know. Tonight, in a house full of people, she'd felt more relaxed, but tomorrow her wish would be granted. There would be just the three of them and she wasn't sure how she was going to cope.

*   *   *

The snow still lay crisp and white on the ground on Christmas morning, and as she gave Jonathan his breakfast Andrina wondered why Drew hadn't appeared as he was usually up first.

As she glanced through the dining-room window she saw him coming up the drive with a purposeful stride and wondered where he'd been at such an early hour. She heard him taking his boots off at the back door and then he was there with them, calm and serene like he'd been when they first met.

Her heart sank. He'd been to the Brewsters', she thought. He'd wanted them to be the first people he saw on Christmas morning. He was looking very pleased with himself so it must have gone down all right.

Please, don't let him ruin the day completely, she prayed, by telling me the split between us is imminent.

There was a spring in his step, and there was peace in the dark blue gaze on hers, so something was right in his world, she decided as she braced herself for what was coming.

It was nothing like she was expecting.

'I've been to see Eamon,' he said, coming to stand beside her.

'What for?'

'I had something to ask him.'

'Oh.'

'Don't you want to know what it was?'

'Should I?'

'Yes. I saw you in his arms the night I was late home from the Brewsters'. I've been in torment ever since. But when I woke up this morning I knew that I had to be certain, that I couldn't face Christmas unless I knew where I stood with you. So I did what I should have done weeks ago and confronted him.'

She was gazing at him, dumbfounded, and he took the spoon out of her hand and continued giving Jonathan his breakfast.

'Oh, no,' she groaned. 'So you thought that he and I were…'

'Yes, I did, and who could blame me?'

'Who indeed,' she murmured. 'And *that* is what's been wrong. I thought it was because you were going back to Tania.'

It was Drew's turn to groan. 'Give me a break! Beside *you* she's superficial, glossy and supremely selfish, and in any case I think there might be a new man in her life. That was what she'd come to tell me the night when you arrived home from hospital unexpectedly.

'The male nurse I engaged to look after Tim seems to have caught her eye, and even though he keeps her in order I don't think he's immune to her charms. But it's *us* we should be talking about, Andrina,' he said softly.

Her eyes were luminous in her pale face as she told him, 'I nearly let Eamon kiss me in a moment of loneliness and misery. You were constantly with Tania and her family and, though I tried not to be, I was jealous.'

He nodded.

'I know. I was to blame for that. It was just that I felt so sorry for Angela and Tim. They were heartbroken over the divorce and on any day of the week Tania is hard work. Then the heart attack, coming out of the blue, floored them completely.

'The night I saw you with Eamon I'd begun to feel that at last my commitment to the Brewsters was easing off and you and I could begin to sort out *our* lives. I was going to ask you to marry me, but what I saw through the kitchen window put the blight on that.

'I'd been desperate to get home to you and Jonathan, but after that I drove to the Grouse and just sat staring into space, telling myself that I'd left it too late. That in my concerns for the Brewsters I'd lost the love of my life. But Eamon has just told me that he never stood a chance with you because…'

He paused and into the silence she said, 'I'm in love with *you* and have been almost from the moment we met. I thought that this was going to be our first and last Christmas together, Drew, and I couldn't bear it.'

He was smiling his special smile.

'So did I. Crazy, aren't we? I never slept last night for thinking about us.'

'Does Tania know how you feel? I suppose she found it strange that someone as nondescript as me should have caught your attention.'

'Caught my attention! Are you kidding? Ever since we met I've been so aware of you I couldn't think straight, and the thought of Jonathan seeing more of Eamon in the future than he did of me was like a knife in my heart. We three are bound together with the bonds of love, Andrina. If you want to give me the best Christmas present ever, say you'll marry me.'

Her face was alight with tenderness, her eyes bright with the promise of what was to come, and he thought, Nondescript? Never!

'Of course I'll marry you,' she told him. She looked down at the rosy, contented baby. 'I love you *both*.'

It was there again, she thought as Drew took her in his arms, the feeling that they weren't alone. That those other presences were close by again, warm and approving.

CHAPTER TEN

EAMON called round during the Christmas pe-
riod and on seeing their faces had said lacon-
ically, 'So it's all come right in the end for
you two?'

'Yes,' Drew told him. 'We're getting married as soon as it can be arranged and I want
you to be my best man.'

His friend laughed. 'Sure. Even though I
had an eye on the bride-to-be myself. But I'll
hide my broken heart on the day and in the
meantime will look for someone else to take
to the ball.'

Andrina smiled across at him, radiant beside
the man she loved.

'What does Tania think about your forth-
coming nuptials?' he asked.

Drew shrugged. 'I don't know and I don't
care. But watch out for the new man in her
life.'

'Really! Who?'

'The male nurse that I hired to care for her father.'

'So all's well that ends well. Everyone finds a true love except me,' Eamon joked.

The wedding plans were under way. One day soon Andrina would walk down the aisle of the village church towards the man she loved and she wouldn't be carrying flowers. She would have Jonathan in her arms, and if there were those who thought it strange she didn't care.

He had brought them together. In caring for his needs, their own had found fulfilment, and as they made their vows to each other they would be surrounded by a circle of caring friends and acquaintances who had taken a fraught stand-in mother into their midst and made her feel as if she belonged.

But before the wedding was the hunt ball on New Year's Eve. Drew was waiting in the hall as he had that other time when Andrina had worn the flame silk dress.

He'd bought the tickets from Serena but at the time had thought the chances small that Andrina might be his partner on the night, yet somehow it had all come right and he was humbly grateful.

He knew that *she* would give him children willingly, brothers and sisters for Jonathan, and soon, when their joint adoption of him came through, the foundation on which they would build their life together would be laid.

Marion had arrived to look after Jonathan and as the New Year beckoned with the promise that had seemed so far away just a short time ago, Andrina came slowly down the stairs.

She'd done the clothes shopping that she'd promised herself in the week between Christmas and New Year and from it had come a long black evening dress, low cut at back and front, high-heeled silver sandals and a matching bag.

And now she was about to join the man she loved, a tall, upright figure, with hair the colour of bright gold, looking just as eye-catching as herself in a dark dinner jacket and trousers, offset by a gleaming white shirt.

'You look *very* beautiful,' he said softly. 'I won't be able to take my eyes off you but, then, I never can.'

As Andrina glowed back at him she knew that the difficult road she'd been forced to set out on the night she'd discovered that Jodie had given birth to a son had brought her to a place where a man and a child were offering her lasting love and contentment.